Jake's hand slid to the top button on his jeans. *Pop!*

"I'll just…" Zoë choked. "I'll just turn around." How the hell could she pose as a newlywed with this guy?

"Uh, you do that…" he mumbled.

She spun around on the changing-room bench so fast she got a splinter in her bottom through her underpants. Blushing, she managed to scramble into the yoga pants, jacket and shoes. Three seconds tops. But she could still hear the sound of his unzipping and rustling and stripping behind her.

Torture, plain and simple.

Fully clothed, Zoë stood. "Ready?" she inquired trying to sound casual, while the image of Jake's naked chest and his hand snaking over his zipper remained branded in her brain.

Her gaze skittered over to his side of the room. *Wowza.*

Jake didn't wear underwear. No tighty whities. No boxers. Nada. And he had a great butt. One of the all-time-great butts. She was going to be haunted by it for the rest of her life.

Zoë flushed. His bare pecs and abs, his butt, *all* within the past five minutes.

How was she ever going to survive this fake honeymoon?

Dear Reader,

As we kick off a special anniversary year for Temptation, I'm thrilled that my three TRUE BLUE CALHOUNS get to share in the excitement!

I love a heroic hero, and I don't think you can do better than men who are willing to take the heat, whether that heat comes from family, job or...love. So I've had a blast working with this trio of brothers who happen to be Chicago cops.

There's big brother Jake, definitely True Blue in *Hot Prospect*. When by-the-book Jake runs into Zoë Kidd, he doesn't realize that she just may be the perfect foil for him. But it's when you throw curves at a straight arrow that the fun begins!

And then you'll meet middle brother Sean, more of a rebel, in *Cut to the Chase*. This detective has an uncanny knack for piercing to the heart of things, but Abra Holloway, on the lam and in trouble, is in no mood to be discovered *or* uncovered.

Last up is baby bro Cooper, who starts *Packing Heat* in order to wrestle with uncompromising FBI agent Violet O'Leary. Violet's handcuffs may just come in handy when it comes to apprehending her man.

Lust, larceny and lawmen in love! What could be more fun?

I hope you'll visit my Web site at www.juliekistler.com to drop me a note or let me know what you think. And I hope you'll fall a little bit in love with the TRUE BLUE CALHOUNS, just as I did!

Best,

Julie Kistler

JULIE KISTLER

HOT PROSPECT

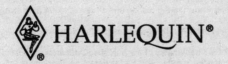

HARLEQUIN®

TORONTO • NEW YORK • LONDON
AMSTERDAM • PARIS • SYDNEY • HAMBURG
STOCKHOLM • ATHENS • TOKYO • MILAN • MADRID
PRAGUE • WARSAW • BUDAPEST • AUCKLAND

ISBN 0-373-69157-2

HOT PROSPECT

This edition published by arrangement with Harlequin Books S.A.

® and TM are trademarks of the publisher. Trademarks indicated with
® are registered in the United States Patent and Trademark Office, the
Canadian Trade Marks Office and in other countries.

Visit us at www.eHarlequin.com

Printed in U.S.A.

1

Jake Calhoun cast a jaded eye at the noisy tourists milling around Chicago's Navy Pier. Lots of people. But not the one he was looking for.

"Where are you, Dad?" he muttered. Damn it, anyway. The last thing Jake needed to be doing this fine summer day was playing spy games with his dad. Especially when he was supposed to be halfway to Wisconsin by now, halfway to an actual vacation, his first in a long time.

But Jake knew the drill. Duty. Loyalty. Responsibility. Those were the words he lived by. So when his father had called and growled, "Meet me at Navy Pier. Ferris wheel. Now," Jake knew his vacation would have to take a back seat.

"Meet him at the Ferris wheel," he grumbled. "What sense does that make?" He ground his hands into the pockets of his jeans, casting a quick glance up at the carefree people laughing and waving as they rolled around on the big ol' wheel. He shook his head. Nope. It made no sense.

"Where is he?" Jake's frown deepened as he cased the pier one more time. This was so strange. And so very unlike his father. Since when did gruff, by-the-book Michael Calhoun, one of five deputy superintendents of police for the city of Chicago, in line to be First Deputy, set up secret meetings at Ferris wheels in the middle of the day? And since when did Michael Calhoun need his son's help for anything more important than painting the garage or driving Grandma Calhoun to the dentist?

None of this made sense. Jake's feeling of foreboding just kept inching higher. And it didn't get any lower when he finally caught sight of his dad. "A coat?" Jake said out loud. "It's got to be a hundred degrees out here, and he's wearing a freakin' trench coat."

Add up the coat, an equally ridiculous hat pulled down over his brow, and his studious attempt to appear nonchalant, and the senior Mr. Calhoun might as well have stenciled "suspicious" on his forehead. He was sitting on a bench, staring out into Lake Michigan, looking like any run-of-the-mill criminal waiting to make a drop. Sheesh. The man was a career cop. He knew better.

"You've even got a briefcase," Jake said in disbelief as he neared his dad. "What are you doing?"

"Ssshhh. Sit down. Don't look at me. Don't let on you know me."

Jake folded his arms over his chest. "Aw, c'mon, Dad. Whatever game you're playing, it's not working."

His father snapped, "Sit down and shut up."

When Michael Calhoun spoke in that tone, his sons knew better than to buck him. Reluctantly Jake took a seat on the other end of the bench, stared out toward the lake and waited for an explanation.

"So?" he tried eventually, feeling like an idiot for not looking at his father as he spoke to him. "Are you going to tell me what this is all about?"

"You in a hurry?"

"I'd really like to get this show on the road and get it over with. Sean and Coop are probably already at the fishing cabin, wondering what the heck happened to me," Jake reminded him.

"Screw your vacation," his dad said sharply. "Your brothers can wait. I got a problem. It needs to be fixed, fast. And you're the only one who can help."

Jake didn't know what to make of that. Sure, he was the oldest son. Sure, everybody knew that he and his father were cut from the same no-nonsense cloth, that they spoke the same language, that when he needed something done, Michael Calhoun turned to Jake first. But that didn't usually involve mysterious meetings at the Navy Pier.

"What exactly is the nature of this problem?" Jake asked, in the same even tone he would've used to question a witness.

"A woman."

Aw, jeez. His father had a problem with a *woman*? That he didn't need to hear.

"Not what you think," his dad said gruffly.

"I wasn't thinking anything."

"You better not be." Exhaling sharply, Michael Calhoun leaned back into the bench. "You should know me better than that."

No response necessary.

"Okay, so here it is. Some chick showed up out of the blue a few weeks ago," he explained tersely, still not looking at Jake. "She says her name is Toni, and she says..."

He trailed off, and Jake had to prompt him. "And? What did she say?"

Finally his father began again. Staring straight ahead, he muttered, "She says she's my daughter."

Jake blinked.

"Yeah, that's right. My *illegitimate* daughter," he finished in a bitter undertone. "What a load of horse manure."

But Jake was still back on *daughter*. Had he fallen into a black hole or something?

"You hear me?" his dad barked.

"Yeah. Some chick named Toni says she's your illegitimate daughter," he said automatically. But when *illegitimate* and Michael Francis Calhoun were spoken in the same breath, the world might as well start spinning on a new axis.

"So this Toni," his father continued, spitting out the name. "She comes to me, and she says her mother was a good-looking con woman I allegedly gave a tumble back in the midseventies." His lip curled into a sour smile. "She says her mom was running some kind of lonely-hearts racket out of the Shakespeare district back when I was still walking a beat, and me, being such a good cop as I was, I caught her red-handed shaking some old guy down. But because she's such a looker, I told her I'd take sexual favors and some cash on the side rather than bust her. Me being such a dirty cop and all."

Jake didn't bother to ask if it was true. He knew his old man as well as he knew himself, and there was just no way. He was sure. Or at least that's what he told himself, quickly, before he had a chance to think about this. The midseventies. When he was barely out of diapers and Sean was on the way. When his parents were poor and happy and as crazy as ever, just starting their lives together, making macramé wall hangings to cover the bare spots and scrounging garage sales for cribs and high chairs. Poor. But honest. Always honest.

The idea that his dad would cheat on his mother with some low-rent con artist was…unthinkable. Wasn't it?

Absolutely. Jake set his jaw. "So I'm guessing this fairy tale didn't end there," he said darkly, waiting for the payoff.

"You guess right." His father tipped up the brim of his crazy hat far enough to wipe sweat off his brow. "I met with this Toni broad a couple of times, just to shake out what the story was. At first I thought, you know, maybe this line of bull is something her mother fed her, and maybe she really does think I'm her old man, so maybe I should let her down easy."

"She got you to feel sorry for her?" Aw, man. Tough guy Michael Calhoun, feeling sorry for a hustler with a ridiculous story. Jake sighed. "So she's that smooth, huh?"

"Yeah, she's smooth all right." He shook his head. "Too smooth. It makes me think that part of her story is true, that her mother probably was a grifter. Trained from the womb, you know?"

"So what happened?"

"So she asks me to come across with a hundred thou," his father went on. "I laugh in her face, like, yeah, your story was entertaining, but not a hundred-grand entertaining. Then she threatens to go to the papers, with 'Love Child Exposes Chicago's Number-Two Cop in Protection Racket' splashed all over the place."

Jake whistled under his breath. "And why didn't you have her arrested? Last time I looked, you were still a cop and blackmail was still a felony. Or do you want me to do it? Is that what you need? Hell, I can get a warrant in about three—"

"Use your head, junior," Michael Calhoun shot back, sending his son a savage look. He hadn't called Jake "junior" in at least ten years. "If she really does go to the papers with this stuff, no matter how ridiculous, they'll pass me over for First Deputy so fast it will make your head spin. They can't promote a guy whose name is all over the papers as part of some alleged sex scandal, even if it is bogus."

"Dad—"

"No, Jake. That promotion is mine, right in my hands. I been waiting for this ever since I joined the department. I'm not screwing it up now because of some little tootsie making up fairy tales."

"But if there's nothing to what she says—"

"I *was* a beat cop then," he insisted, "in the Shakespeare district, right where she says. We *did* have a rash of complaints about a beautiful woman fleecing men in the area, and we never caught her. Her story sounds just plausible enough to cause me a whole lot of trouble."

"But you can do DNA testing," Jake put in. "You can prove she's not your daughter."

"After I'm raked through the papers for months," his father said acidly. "And it's not just the promotion. We're talking your mother here. You know her. With all this stuff in the papers, she'd either haul off and kill me herself or just have a stroke, long before I got the DNA results back."

"Mom." Jake swallowed. He hadn't thought about her reaction. He loved his mother dearly, but she wasn't what you'd call a clearheaded, rational person when it came to her husband. She was hotheaded and had a jealous streak a mile wide. Always had. Mom, confronted with these accusations...ouch.

"And now, as if it couldn't get any worse, the girl has disappeared." Michael Calhoun shook his head.

"What do you mean, disappeared?"

"I mean she set up another meeting," he said grimly. "A week ago. I was sitting out there on my park bench, waiting for her. But she never showed."

"You think she got scared off and took a powder?"

His father shrugged. "I don't know what to think. I put Vince on it, and he can't find a trace."

"Vince?" Jake rolled his eyes skyward. This just kept getting worse. Vince had been his father's right-hand man on the force for twenty-five years. He was loyal to a fault, a good guy from the get-go, but not exactly the sharpest knife in the drawer, even on his best days *before* he went deaf and had one knee and a hip replaced. Not exactly an ace investigator. "Dad, Vince retired six or seven years ago. What are you doing bringing him in on this?"

"He's my friend. I can trust him," he replied. "You got a problem with that?"

"No, of course not, but..." But now the leading candidate for First Deputy Superintendent of Police was not only conducting some kind of secret personal investigation concerning allegations of blackmail and professional misconduct, but he was also involving other people. Other people like Vince, who could stumble into all sorts of trouble. Carefully Jake asked, "You're not using department resources to do this, are you?"

All he got in response was a very dark look.

"Okay, forget I asked." Jake sighed. "But if she's gone, why isn't this over?"

"'Cause I'm worried, okay? What if she's laying low till she can blow the story? Or plotting some new strategy? Or something worse?" He shuddered. "I need to know. Now."

"And what is it you want me to do?" Jake asked slowly, dreading the answer.

"I know you've got a couple of weeks off. And your profile is a lot lower than mine." He paused. Jake knew what was coming. Not that that made it any more appetizing. "I got a real bad feeling about this, like she's out there somewhere waiting to strike. Or that she was consorting with a more dangerous class of perp and got herself offed or something. You gotta find her and make this go away before she can cause any more trouble."

"Dad, I..." *I don't want to get knee-deep in this mess. I want to go on vacation. I want to go fishing with my brothers, as planned.* But he was the responsible one, the one who never said no. Too late to start having the good sense to decline now.

"Did you think about asking Sean?" he tried, clutching at one last straw. "He's the detective, not me. He's the one with..." What had the papers said? Sean had cracked a couple of supposedly uncrackable cases and gained a reputation rather quickly. Sean, who never wanted to be a cop in the first place, had been promoted to detective in spite of himself. Jake smiled. Funny how that turned out. He couldn't quite keep the sarcasm out of his voice when he said, "According to the press releases, Sean's the one with the uncanny instinct for the truth."

"I'm not asking Sean," his father said quickly. "You're my boy, Jakie. I know how you think. Not that seat-of-the-pants baloney like Sean. You're like me. Play by the rules." He tapped his temple with one finger. "Think it through."

Yeah, I know. That's me. Play by the rules. Jake, number two on the list of True Blue Calhouns, right behind his dad.

"And I don't want you involving either of your brothers or your mother in this," Michael Calhoun continued, looking very fierce all of a sudden. "Nobody knows. This is between you and me. You got that?"

"Yeah." *Between you, me, Vince and the missing tootsie,* he thought bleakly. Like he would really want to share this information with anyone, anyway. The more he thought about it, the more he realized Dad was right on that point. No way he could tell Sean or Cooper that their father was being blackmailed by some scam artist claiming to be their illegitimate half sister. Since Sean and their old man had never seen eye-to-eye, the middle Calhoun son would probably get all moody and upset on Mom's behalf, while the youngest, Cooper, would no doubt think it was a hoot and then want to find this girl and hang out and have a few beers or something. Sean would growl about how the old man couldn't be trusted, while Coop would be going, *A new sister. Cool!*

Taking Dad's side was, as always, left to Jake.

"So what have you got to go on? Real name? Record? Anything?"

His father scrambled to open the briefcase. "She was pretty cagey, so I haven't got much. Never could get prints or anything to run. But I had Vince take some pictures the last time I met with her."

He handed over a couple of blurry shots, partially obscured by tree branches and leaves, showing two people sitting on what looked like a park bench. As far as Jake could tell, one of the figures was his father, in the same getup he was wearing now, while the woman sitting next to him had a frizzy mop of platinum blond hair and dark sunglasses. There were a few more pictures, showing her as she walked away from the bench and closer to the photographer, but they were equally lousy.

"Vince losing his eyesight now, too?" Jake asked, squinting at the out-of-focus photos.

"What?"

"Nothing." Jake flipped back through the stack. The only one that appeared to be completely in focus was taken from the waist down. Oh, great. He had a crystal-clear view of her feet.

The photos revealed that she was medium height, curvy enough to attract a lot of male attention, and trashy enough to be tottering in high-heeled sandals with scruffy, way-too-tight, way-too-low-cut blue jeans. Toe rings. Nail polish. Sparkly hooker shoes with straps that crisscrossed over her ankle. Other than that...she could've been anyone.

He frowned. "Is this it?" He'd never find her with nothing more than a few fuzzy photographs taken from behind a tree and one sharp shot of her legs.

"Vince got somebody to run what we had through the system on the sly, but it came up empty. I looked for matches with the old files from the seventies, too, but that led nowhere."

"Dad, I don't think there's any way—"

"I got one other lead," his father interrupted. "The last time I met her, about a week ago, when Vince took the pictures, I told him to stick with her and see where she went. He followed her to..."

He dipped back into the briefcase, holding up a sheet from a memo pad. "Okay, here it is. Vince tailed her to someplace called Red Sails Specialty Tours, a fancy travel agency on Michigan Avenue. He said he sneaked in behind her, all casual, and pretended he was inter-ested in cruises, you know, looking at the brochures, so he could eavesdrop."

That was when his dad actually cracked a smile, and Jake could see why. It was pretty funny imagining grumpy old Vince shuffling into some travel agency and peering through his thick bifocals at the Caribbean cruise brochures.

"He hear anything good?"

"Yeah." Once again, Michael Calhoun consulted the bits of paper in his briefcase. "He heard her book tickets on a tour that leaves from O'Hare tomorrow. Two tickets on something called the Explorer's Journey. Vince said it cost a bundle and she paid cash, right then and there."

"So maybe you're not the only game she's playing? Maybe she squeezed some money out of some other mark and she's blowing town on her take. Or maybe she's playing a lonely-hearts racket of her own, and she conned the mark into taking her on some fancy trip." He considered. "Tomorrow, huh?"

"Yeah. That's why this is such a rush." His lips pressed into a narrow line. "This should be easy, Jake. Piece of cake. All you have to do is go to this Red Sails joint, book yourself on to the same tour, get next to her, and get the goods."

"You want me to take her tour?" Jake echoed. "Can't I just show up at O'Hare, arrest her, and be done with it?"

"You can't arrest her! Haven't you been listening?" He shook his head impatiently. "You have to stay undercover, Jake, get next to her, find out who else she's scammed, what she plans to do next. Maybe we can take her down for something else and get rid of her without bringing me into it at all."

Jake didn't seriously think this woman was his father's illegitimate daughter. Not for a second. He narrowed his eyes, wondering about his father's motives. How much of this had to do with his dad wanting to avoid a scandal? And how much with pride?

Did Deputy Superintendent Michael Calhoun want little Miss Toni taken down because he truly thought she was dangerous? Or because she'd dared to mess with *him*?

"So you seriously want me to sign up for some..." What had he called it? "Explorer's Journey?" Jake glanced down at the last photo, the one from the waist down. "She doesn't look like the type to be climbing Mount Kilimanjaro. Not in those shoes."

His father remained unamused. "Just do it, Jake. Sign up for the tour, figure out what the deal is, make her go away. I'll foot the bill. But this is your chance to come through for me, Jake. I need you."

Way to push all the right buttons, old man. Jake really didn't want to sign up for a tour at the last minute, just to follow some probably half-cocked lead to nowhere. Staring out into the gray-blue water of Lake Michigan, he ran a hand through his hair, letting himself imagine for a second that he was going to say no. He conjured up one last cozy image of the fishing cabin in Wisconsin, of his brothers, a cooler full of beer, a nice big lake trout frying up in a pan...and then he banished it all. The cabin, the boys, the beer, the fish, all of it.

Bottom line—when his dad asked, Jake responded. They all knew that. *This is your chance to come through for me, Jake. I need you.*

He was the oldest, the responsible one, the one Dad could depend on. He glanced over at his father, sitting there waiting for an answer. Jake nodded. "Yeah, okay. I'll do it."

IF THE EXPLORER'S JOURNEY, whatever the heck it was, left tomorrow, he didn't have much time. He quickly left messages on both Sean and Cooper's cell phones that they shouldn't expect him in Wisconsin. For once, he was happy to reach voice mail. At least this way he didn't have to offer anything more in the way of explanations. Then he headed over to the Red Sails travel agency.

There was only one clerk working this Friday afternoon, and she seemed quite frazzled as she tried to deal with ringing telephones and a beeping fax machine. "I'm new," she said into the phone about seventeen times, her voice trilling with increasing panic. He heard her wail "Please don't yell at me!" another five or six times.

Not a good sign. Jake tried to catch her eye as he lounged there in front of her desk, but she kept holding a "wait a minute, I can't talk to you yet" finger in the air and jabbering on into her headset about something to do with a cruise ship and stranded passengers. "I'm new," she tossed in yet again. "Please don't yell at me!"

Feeling more than a tad irritable, Jake let his eyes wander over the posters of Jamaica and Tahiti, hoping against hope that if he had to be on it, the Explorer's Journey was at least headed somewhere good. Maybe these explorers went in for scuba diving or island hopping. Hawaiian shirts and mai tais with little umbrellas in them might be fun. Man, he needed a vacation.

As the girl behind the desk hyperventilated into her phone, Jake hunted through the racks of brochures, looking for clues, but there was nothing there about any Explorer's Journey. "With my luck, it'll be the North Pole," he muttered.

At last, she punched a button on her phone, took off her headset, heaved a big sigh and stood up. "Can I help you?" she asked doubtfully, as if she already knew that whatever it was he wanted, she wouldn't have it.

"Hi," he offered with a smile, trying his best to work around his annoyance level. "Bad day, huh?"

"I'm new," she blurted out, waving her hands helplessly. "The computer isn't working, the other agent had to run off to find someone to fix the computers, and there's a whole cruise ship full of Beanie Baby collectors stranded in Puerta Vallarta with possible dysentery." Fear colored her face as she stared up at him. "You won't tell anybody, will you? I mean, if they do have dysentery, it may not be the fault of Red Sails or the cruise. It could be a coincidence."

"Uh-huh."

She started to sniffle, her voice rising, tears brimming in her eyes. "I unplugged the phone. I had to. I don't know what to tell them. It's not my fault! I wasn't even here when their cruise was arranged."

"I'm sure they'll understand." He leaned in closer, nabbing and handing her a tissue from the box on her desk. He tried to think of something nice to say. "Look on the bright side—if they're stranded together, at least they have something to talk about."

"Well, there is that." She stared at him. "Did you need something? Not a cruise, I hope."

"I'm actually not sure what it is. Something called the Explorer's Journey?"

Dabbing at her eyes, she blinked three or four times, as if that would help jump-start her brain. She shook her head. "I've never heard of it."

Afraid even the slightest impatience would knock her over the edge into a collapse, he tried to ooze nonthreatening, nice-guy vibes. He was usually pretty good at that. "I know someone who booked this Explorer's Journey from this agency. Is there somewhere you can look for information about it?"

"The computers are down," she said in a quavery tone.

He crooked his thumb at the filing cabinets lining the wall behind her. "How about your files?"

She scrunched up her face, staring vacantly at him.

"They look alphabetical. Maybe the cabinet that says *E-F-G* on it," Jake suggested. "*E* for Explorers?"

"Oh." She stumbled back there and pulled open the top drawer. "Hmm...these are mostly European tours. What did you say it was again?"

"Explorer's Journey."

"Is that Europe?" she asked, giving him a hopeful glance.

"I don't know."

She sighed again. "I don't see anything." After poking through those files for a few more minutes, she continued on to the second drawer, fumbled through a few more folders, let her shoulders sag in defeat, turned back, saw the look on Jake's face, and—just at the point where he was ready to leap over the desk and start looking himself—reluctantly returned to her halfhearted search. "Nope. I don't see anything...oh, wait. What did you say it was? Explorer's Journey. Here it is."

Jake held his breath. Although she seemed astonished to have located it, she actually had a file folder in her hands. The label pasted to the front really did identify it as Explorer's Journey. She slid it onto her desk and opened it up, carefully, slowly flipping the pages over one at a time.

"Is there a brochure or anything in there? Any information?"

"No. Just the registration pages. They look really full. It must be popular." She continued to turn pages at the speed of mud. Slow mud. "There's one a month, I guess. Here's March... April..."

Could she be any slower, even if she really, really

tried? "I need July," he reminded her, holding himself back from snatching the file away from her. "It's supposed to leave tomorrow."

"Here it is. July." Peering down at it, she smoothed the page with one hand, blocking his view, neatly detaching a piece of pink memo paper clipped to the corner and setting it aside. "Oh, that's too bad. All the spaces are filled."

"Can't you add me as an extra?" How hard could it be? He could see, even upside down, that there were names on all the lines, neatly divided into two columns. A quick count told him there were forty people scheduled to be on this trip. So what difference would it make if they went to forty-one?

"Oh, no, I couldn't do that." She turned the page around, pointing to the instructions scrawled across the top. Someone had written *No Extras! No Waiting List!* in big, bold letters.

Jake ignored that little problem for the moment, glancing down the list now that he had a chance to see it right side up, scanning for possibilities. One Antoinette, a Tonya, a Tori, and two names that just used *T* as a first initial. Plus there was one listed under the last name Antonini. The woman he was looking for could be any of them. Or none, if she had a pile of aliases.

"So you see I can't add you," she continued. "It's very clear that I'm not allowed to do that even if I did know how to register you for this trip, which I don't, because the computers are down and I can't even look up what it costs or anything."

She painstakingly reattached the pink memo and its paper clip and then moved to close the folder, but Jake laid a hand on top of hers. "Isn't there any other way you can let me in on this tour? Anybody else I could contact? Any other source of info? Anything?"

"Not that I would know about..." Looking even more unhappy and put-upon, she glanced back at the beeping fax machine and blinking phone. "Here." She shoved the folder at him. "You look."

He flipped through it again, noting no contact name, no info, no help. But then he saw the pink memo attached to the June sheet, and his eyes caught the word "cancel." Holding up the sheet of pink paper, he read aloud, "'Zoë Kidd tried to cancel 6/12. Told her no cancel/no refund but would pass on her name if anyone wanted to buy her spot.'" He raised an eyebrow. "What about this? Can I buy her spot?"

"Oh. Well. I don't know. I guess you can try," she said with a shrug. "It's nothing to do with me."

Then she wandered back to the fax machine as Jake considered this stroke of luck.

The tour was full, but Zoë Kidd wanted to cancel and had a space available to give. For the first time since he'd heard his father's unlikely tale, Jake Calhoun began to smile.

Zoë Kidd. She wanted to cancel. He wanted her spot.

Sounded like a match made in heaven.

2

ZOË BREATHED in the scent of sandalwood from her meditation candles. Lovely. Soothing. Cleansing.

Sitting there on her new purple yoga mat, she maneuvered her legs into the full lotus position, balancing her elbows on her knees and curling her index fingers and thumbs into the proper O's.

She had a terrible impulse to sneeze, and she decided she probably shouldn't have lit all eleven candles at the same time. The waves of sandalwood were really kind of overpowering. But eleven was her lucky number. And now that she had gotten herself twisted like a pretzel into the full lotus, she really didn't want to extract herself just to blow out a few candles.

She closed her eyes and concentrated. Lovely. Soothing. Cleansing. *Breathe the sandalwood,* she ordered herself. *And don't think. Whatever you do, don't think.*

Yeah, right. Don't think about the fact that today was supposed to have been her wedding day and tomorrow was supposed to have been the day that she and that snake Wylie left for their honeymoon on the Explorer's Journey.

He was the one who'd wanted to get married, damn it. She was perfectly happy to live together. Or not even, just to coexist peacefully in their separate apartments. But *no.* He'd insisted they had to be married. And she'd said, *But we're not ready for that. We have* issues. And he'd said, *But, hon, I want to be a real couple, like regular people. I want to build a real life together.* Which made her heart melt a little, just like he knew it would. *If we have issues,* Wylie had told her, so sincere, *we can work through them.*

Which should've been a hint right there that Wylie was off his rocker at that particular moment, because he was *so* not the work-through-your-issues type. But then, like the dim bulb she was, she had been thrilled to hear him finally admit that, yes, there were things that he needed to improve—because this was sure as heck the first time he'd ever said *that,* seeing as how he was con- vinced he was perfect. So she'd said, quite sternly, actu- ally, *Yes, Wylie, I will marry you, but only if we go on the Ex- plorer's Journey for our honeymoon because I just saw it on* Oprah. *Newlyweds only, all about communication, harmony, trust, blah, blah, blah, all the things we have trouble with. It'll be the perfect way to work through some things, right there, right then. And we can begin our married life as full and equal partners, communicating, harmonizing, trusting.*

Had there been a funny light of terror in his eyes when he'd agreed? Or was that just hindsight?

"Did you ever have any intention of doing the Ex- plorer's Journey with me?" she asked out loud. "And if not, why the hell couldn't you say so before I paid for the damn thing?"

Well, there she was, with her eyes wide-open, not calm or relaxed or *cleansed* at all. And her right ankle was starting to kill her where it was mashed between her other leg and her lap, not to mention the fact that the backs of both thighs were plastered to her mat.

"Ow…" She wrenched herself out of her lotus posi- tion, peeling the sticky mat away from her skin. She was positively dripping with sweat in this hateful apart- ment. It was so humid, without a hint of a breeze. And all those candles were making it worse. "I shouldn't be wearing shorts. But it's too hot for long pants! And I could've afforded air-conditioning if I hadn't paid for that stupid Explorer's Journey. They can just stuff their no-cancellation policy."

Well, she wasn't feeling particularly meditative, was she? Maybe a few rounds with her tarot cards would help her get in touch with her higher power and stop all the angsting already.

Refastening one reddish-brown braid back over the top of her head, she slicked the moisture off her forehead with the back of one hand, swearing again, louder this time. Stupid, stupid Wylie for being too chicken to be part of a real couple. Stupid, stupid Zoë for ever thinking he was worth it in the first place. She'd ignored her cards on that one, when they kept throwing her the Prince of Hearts every time she asked about Wylie. Everyone knew the Prince of Hearts meant an Inconstant Suitor. Which described Wylie exactly.

"How can you respect a man who doesn't know his own mind?" she groused. "I should've believed the cards."

Zoë picked herself up off the ground and started rooting around on her bookshelves for her pack of Enchanted Tarot Cards. They had beautiful pictures and she really did find them soothing as long as they kept that nasty Inconstant Suitor card to themselves. The deck was on the bottom shelf, and she was bent over, reaching for the last card, which had slipped to the very back of the shelf, when she heard the clomp of footsteps coming up the stairs to her apartment. She paused. Maybe a new student, she thought. Which would be a very good thing, because she needed the extra money now that she'd spent every last dime she had on the non-refundable Explorer's Journey.

She raised her head, planning to call out to whoever it was to just come on in, but she lifted up too quickly, cracking her head squarely on the next shelf.

"Yeow!" she cried, stumbling back, scattering a waterfall of tarot cards like something out of Alice in Wonderland. There was only one card left in her hand.

She rubbed the back of her head, almost slipping as she stepped on one of the slick cards on the floor. She groaned. It had to be bad karma to drop all your tarot cards. "I guess I'd better pick 'em up." She slid the one card she still had into the back pocket of her shorts and bent down to get the deck back together before the potential student walked in and saw the mess. But when she bent over, she started to feel really dizzy. "I must've bumped it harder than I thought," she whispered, stretching her fingers to her toes, letting her head hang down to the floor while she recovered her equilibrium. It was at that point she heard the door open behind her.

"Come—" she began, but she only got the one syllable out.

"Stop, police!" a very male voice announced. "Don't move!"

"What? Stay where I am?" Bent over with her backside in the air? Frozen to the spot, she stared at him through her legs. Good God, he had a gun! Kinda cute, but scary, with both his arms outstretched and that creepy gun pointed mostly at the floor. But he wasn't wearing a uniform. Man. Gun. "Are you really a cop? Show me your badge!" she screamed.

He immediately pulled out a shield and flashed it at her. Okay, good. So he really was a cop.

"Were you shouting at someone?" he asked in a

calmer voice, relaxing his stance a little as he surveyed the empty room.

"No. Myself, maybe," she offered. "I hit my head and then I dropped my cards and...do I have to stay like this? All the blood is running to my head. I was already dizzy and now I feel like I'm going to faint."

He backed off, putting the gun away, thank goodness, shutting her front door quietly. "No, no, get up. Please. Whatever. Sorry."

"Whew." Slowly, carefully, Zoë straightened, lifting a hand to her head. Yes, she was still a little light-headed, but not too bad. Meanwhile, his gaze was positively glued to her bottom. It was probably not his fault, she allowed, considering how brief her shorts were, especially when she'd been bent over like that. What was the poor thing supposed to look at?

But how humiliating. The only cute guy who'd been in her apartment for weeks, and he barged in while she was woozy, sweaty, upside down and had half her butt exposed. She ventured a glance his way. He didn't look too upset by the short-shorts problem. In fact, he looked positively...intrigued. Zoë swallowed. Yep, he was still looking at her.

After tugging the edge of her shorts down, she pushed a few tendrils of hair back into her braids, blew on her face and hoped she wasn't too flushed. Oh, forget it. She looked hideous. There was no point in trying to spruce herself up at this point. The light she'd seen in his eyes must be her imagination. No man in the world sent out vibes of interest to a woman who looked like *this*.

Careful to avoid all the spilled cards, she edged around so that at least her front side was facing him. And then she gave him a real once-over. Okay, twice. He knew she was looking. She knew he knew. And she didn't care. Because the view was that good.

Light brown hair, cut short. Good, clean jawline. Blue eyes. Very blue. There was a sort of speculative, suspicious look in those eyes she found oddly attractive. That and his mouth. He had these quirky lips, kind of narrow and clever, fuller on the bottom. She liked the look of those lips. A lot.

He was tall, maybe six foot one or two, with broad shoulders, and a real *presence*. Nothing she could put her finger on but... Alive. Vital. Rooted. Right here. Right now. He looked like the kind of guy you would run to when a tornado just blew your house away and you didn't have a thing left in the world and you didn't care because you had *him*.

Zoë's eyes met his. Good Lord, he was cute. In a very traditional, button-down, authority-figure way, of course, which was not her type at all. *So* incredibly and completely not her type. He'd pulled a gun on her, for goodness' sake!

Now if he would only stop sending her those sizzling glances. They made her want to run to him and tackle him. Which was probably a very bad thing. She vowed to do a better job of being immune to whatever he was sending out.

She lifted her chin. "Why in the world did you come barreling in like that? Pointing that thing at me!"

"I heard thumps and a scream. The door was open, there was a definite haze in here, and it smelled like marijuana." He looked kind of grouchy as he scanned the room again. "How many candles are you burning? And why?"

"I don't think how many candles I'm burning is any of

your business. And it's sandalwood, not marijuana. Jeez Louise, what kind of cop are you?"

"I thought there might be a burglary in progress, or maybe some kind of drug party gone bad," he explained curtly. "That does not smell like sandalwood. You're not burning the candles to cover the pot smell, are you? Is anyone else here? Is there a back door?"

"No, no, and no. I'm alone. The candles are supposed to be good for meditation. I don't have a back door." She took a sniff. Good grief. He was right. It didn't smell like sandalwood. No wonder she wasn't getting any calmer. "I'm going to have to have a talk with the lady at the New Age store downstairs. She swore these were sandalwood."

"Uh-huh."

"Well, it's true." She tried to plant her hands on her hips and look menacing, but her hand hit the smooth, hard edge of the tarot card poking out of her back pocket. Hmm...one card in her pocket. If one fell out or otherwise distanced itself from the pack, that was supposed to be significant. She pulled it out of her pocket and glanced down.

"That's odd," she murmured. It was a swirling pink card with two pretty swans outlined by a heart, with two tiny kissing cupids at the top. The two of hearts.

The True Love card.

Her heart did a little flip, but she ignored it. Instead she glared at the card in her hand. Talk about adding insult to injury. Even her tarot cards were mocking her.

So where was this True Love supposed to pop up? Between her and...

"Hello?" the cute cop interrupted. "If you're done playing cards, I need to talk to you."

Him? She gulped. Those beautiful blue eyes were staring at her, burning more steadily than all eleven candles. Her heart started to thump, beating to the most bizarre rhythm. *True love. True love. True love.* She felt all tingly, and her face was flushed with heat. What was wrong with her?

It was probably just the effect of too many aromatic candles, infecting her brain. Or maybe she'd hit her head harder than she realized. There was no romantic glow here at all. Just smoke and humidity.

She fanned herself with the two of hearts, using her other hand to pluck the neckline of her damp leotard away from her skin. Anything to generate some air. *Cool down, chill out,* she told herself. But she didn't feel remotely cool or chilly.

Especially when his gaze seemed to catch and hold there on her chest. His eyes widened. She swallowed, surreptitiously casting a quick look down to see what he was staring at. Overheated Zoë. Wet leotard. Breasts that might as well have been bare in that thin, moist top, her nipples peaking against the slippery, wet fabric.

Uh-oh. She dropped the True Love card like a shot, kicking it out of the way as she quickly wrapped her arms over her front and turned away.

She was not, as it happened, all that shy about her body. She was used to leading her dance class in a skimpy leotard all the time. But this felt different. It felt like...dancing naked in front of a complete stranger. Even worse, it felt like dancing naked, totally on purpose and with one seductive reason, in front of your lover.

She couldn't handle it. Pulling her top out in front, hoping she looked nonchalant, she unstuck it and flapped it harder, trying to dry herself off. But when she hazarded a glance back around at him, his gaze met hers, blazing like a beacon, and it was like, *Pow! Kazam! Major meltdown happening here!*

What the...?

Sometimes she had feelings about people, or even a little intuition, but nothing as overwhelming and *hot* as this. She didn't just get an aura from him. No, this was like a laser beam, searing her all the way to the soul. *I know him,* she thought, shocked at the very idea. *I know him!*

He blinked, looking just as surprised as she was. *Jake.* One minute she had no idea who he was, and the next his name was right there in her brain, clear as day. His name was Jake. How did she know that?

Zoë took a step backward. This couldn't be happening. One tarot card did not a lover make. And yet there was some kind of cosmic attraction going on here, and they both knew it.

She wasn't used to this instant-electricity thing. She wasn't used to looking at a guy for five minutes, thinking about laser beams and naked dancing, and totally wanting to jump him.

She was coming undone.

"Oh, dear! Well, I, uh..." She put a hand to her forehead, attempting to find something else in the room that needed her attention. But there wasn't anything there. "The candles...it's *so* hot in here. Maybe it's the candles."

Behind her, he cleared his throat. "You really should blow those out," he said stiffly. "They're a fire hazard."

As she moved to blow out the nearest two, she stopped, glancing at him over her shoulder, her gaze skittering away again. She tried to make a joke, anything to puncture this bizarre mood. "So tell me, did you come here to bust me for excess candle burning?"

"No, actually, I came because..." He stopped. Sounding even more unsettled than she felt, he continued, "I'm looking for Zoë Kidd. Is that you?"

"Yes. But I didn't..." She was planning on saying she didn't have any reason to need a police officer when it hit her.

If there was a cop looking for her, there could only be one reason. Her shoulders slumped. *Wylie.* He'd probably run up a few too many parking tickets again. The very thought of Wylie was like a pitcher of cold water poured over her head.

Wylie equaled bad taste in men. Wylie equaled terrible judgment. Wylie equaled defeat.

After quickly dousing the remaining candles, Zoë went back to pick up the rest of her tarot cards, trying hard to ignore Mr. Cute Cop. She made a point of retrieving the two of hearts and jamming it back into the middle of the pack before she stacked the whole deck neatly on the bookshelf. "If this is about Wylie, I broke up with him almost a month ago. Any trouble he's in is his problem, not mine. So if he said I would bail him—"

"No, it has nothing to do with him. I need you."

Yeah, well, I need you, too, Jake. I dumped my boyfriend. I'm lonely. I'm bored. And you are one good-looking man.

Looking over at him, trying to make herself behave, she still felt that incredible heat. She still felt like stripping naked and leaping into his arms. She licked her bottom lip. *I need you for a few good rolls on my sticky mat...*

"What did you say?"

"Me? Nothing. Not a thing." What, could he hear her thoughts now? His name suddenly popped into her head as if it always been there and now he could mind-read? This was getting spooky. She stuck a stray tendril of her hair back into the braids wrapped over the top of her head. "And what did you need with me?"

"Okay. Right. Let's just...cut to the chase."

He clenched his jaw, and she thought, *Wow, that is one nice jaw. Do you think he would care if I touched it?* before she regained the use of her brain and paid attention to his words again. *Concentrate, Zoë. Concentrate.* Why was it so incredibly hot in this room?

"You booked a place on the Explorer's Journey, right?"

Zoë blinked. "You're here because of the Explorer's Journey?"

"The travel agency said the roster is full," he explained. "I want to buy your spot."

"You want to...?" He didn't seem like the type. At all. But then she got the picture. Talk about your pitcher of cold water.

Zoë was not a stupid woman. She saw the handwriting on the wall. Mr. Cute Cop obviously had a *Mrs.* Cute Cop stashed at home, and the two of them wanted to go on the Explorer's Journey. Newlyweds only, after all. Newlyweds who wanted to work on their communication skills, both in and out of bed. Given Mr. Cute Cop's rather terse communication skills, as well as the heat emanating from his hard body, she could see why Mrs. Cute Cop would feel the need to take him on that particular trip.

"So you'll sell me your ticket?" he asked.

"Sure," she declared, trying to work up some enthusiasm.

Shaking her head, she rose from the floor, crossing to the desk where she'd stuck the travel packet. How silly was she? She'd gone from entertaining the mad notion that he was her karmic one-and-only True Love to figuring out he was someone else's new husband, all in three seconds. So much for her psychic visions. She knew his name. How come she didn't get the married part?

She glanced up. Funny, he wasn't wearing a ring. And she did not get a married vibe from him at all, especially when you factored in his eyes being fastened to a variety of her body parts ever since he got here. Yes, he was a guy and guys did that kind of thing. But he just didn't seem the type to be newly married *and* looking around, and she usually trusted her intuition when it came to guy matters.

Zoë considered this mystery for several seconds, before deciding there wasn't anything she could do about it, and it was just too aggravating to contemplate. If he, his wife and his wandering eyes wanted to throw themselves into a newlywed encounter group, that was their business.

Wagging the Explorer's Journey folio at him, she plastered on a wide, chipper smile. "This sucker was expensive and I'll be glad to get it off my hands. But you do know it leaves first thing in the morning, right? Do you and your wife have time to pack?"

"I'm not married," he said quickly.

She knew it! There was totally an unmarried aura just hovering all around him. She was thrilled for a second, realizing that her instincts had been right. But then she had another depressing thought.

"Oh." Zoë crossed her arms over her chest. "So you're taking your girlfriend. I thought you could only do the program if you were married. Although now that I think about it, doing it *before* you get married sounds like a much better idea. Or are you planning to just lie and tell them you're married? Not that it matters to me."

Slowly he asked her, "Why would I need to be married?"

"Because..." That gave her pause. He wanted to go on the Explorer's Journey and he didn't know? She narrowed her eyes. Feeling very shrewd, she inquired, "You don't know what the Explorer's Journey is, do you?"

He just looked at her for a long moment.

"You don't!" she exclaimed. "I can tell you don't." Now this was getting interesting. Zoë advanced on him, her eyes wide with curiosity. "Why do you want to go if you don't know what it is? Is your girlfriend making you go?"

"I don't have a girlfriend," he said reluctantly.

Yes! Zoë felt like doing happy dances. She refrained. But she felt the triumph in her heart. She wasn't wrong about him! Single, single, single!

But if it wasn't for a relationship, then why did he want to go? "Is it for work? You have to go for like, official *police* reasons?"

"No." Other than that, he kept his mouth shut. His lips looked even more intriguing pressed together like that.

Zoë was nothing if not persistent when it came to mysteries and puzzles. She drew a little closer. "You don't think I'm going to hand over my tickets unless you tell me why you need to go, do you?"

"I'm not at liberty to discuss this with you," he said tersely. "And you said *tickets*, plural. I only need one."

"Well, you certainly can't go by yourself." All by his lonesome? Mr. Cute Cop hadn't done his homework, had he? She tapped the ticket packet against her chin.

"Why exactly is it a problem if I go by myself?" he asked. He was starting to sound a little testy. "What were you talking about before, about having to be married, or taking a girlfriend? What is this all about? What kind of exploration are we talking? North Pole? Mount Saint Helen's? What?"

"Forgive me," she said thoughtfully, looking him up and down, "but you don't seem like the explorer type."

"Neither do you."

She shrugged, not at all concerned. "Are you going to tell me why you want to go? Or am I going to hold on to my tickets *and* my explanation of just what exactly the Explorer's Journey is?"

Finally he muttered, "It's none of your business, but the truth is... I have to find someone. I have reason to believe she'll be on this tour."

"She? So you have to find a woman." Zoë was very close now, looking right up into his face, and she found this all fascinating. Her mind was working a mile a minute, considering possibilities. Not married. No girlfriend. Dying to go on the Explorer's Journey to find a particular woman. "Is she your ex-girlfriend or something? She dumped you, hooked up with some other guy, got married, and now she's going on the Explorer's Journey with him. And you want to follow her. Why? Are you stalking her? Maybe you think you can get her away from the other guy? Or are you just torturing yourself?"

"You're giving me a headache," he said between clenched teeth.

"Oh, c'mon." She jiggled his elbow. "Stalker? Win her back? Torment yourself?"

"None of the above. And why do you care?" he asked darkly. "I need to find her. She may be on this tour. That's it."

"Well, you can't go by yourself."

"Why not?" he snapped.

Zoë beamed up at him. "Because...if you must know..." She let her voice trail off. She was kind of enjoying letting him dangle now that she knew he was single. He was so very cute and his impatience only made him cuter somehow.

"Yes?" he prompted.

"Okay, okay. I guess you don't watch *Oprah*, do you? Because the Explorer's Journey has been all over *Oprah*. How to describe it?" She bit her lip. "Hmmm... I guess the closest I can come is to say it's a kind of a combination of group therapy and a honeymoon."

His eyebrows arched. "Group therapy? Honeymoon?"

Taking in his expression, she said slyly, "That's right. And let me tell you, Jake, I can't see you enjoying either all by yourself."

He recovered quickly. "Yeah, but... somebody must go solo on this thing." He sent her a quick glance. "People break up all the time. But, hey, they already paid the money, so why shouldn't one of them go ahead and take the vacation? Like you. You broke up with your boyfriend, right? A few weeks ago."

"He was my fiancé. Ex-fiancé. And that's why I wanted to cancel my tickets. I sure wasn't planning to go without him."

Pacing farther away, over near the bookcase, Zoë shook her head, hoping they could change the subject. She did not need to be thinking about her lamented love life right now. She picked up the deck of tarot cards again, absently shuffling them.

His eyes measured her. Gruffly, in a way that told her it had nothing to do with the Explorer's Journey, he asked, "So when were you supposed to get married?"

"Well...today."

"Oh." He lifted his shoulders in a very small shrug. "Sorry. That's a tough break."

"Yeah." Zoë kept her mouth shut. There was no way she wanted to discuss that at this moment. *Just don't be nice about it, will you, Jake? Don't be nice to me. I don't want to lose control and melt all over you.* Turning back, she asked, "So, Jake, tell me, are you going on this tour or not?"

He started to nod, but stopped suddenly. "That's the second time you've called me Jake. But I never told you my name."

Uh-oh. She covered quickly. "You must have."

He shook his head.

"Wasn't it on that identification thing next to your badge?" she tried.

"My ID was half a room away from you and you were upside down at the time."

She bit her lip. "I have good eyesight."

"Must be X-ray vision." His expression was very guarded. "So how did you know my name?"

Zoë shrugged, shuffling the cards with more enthusiasm. "Listen, it doesn't matter. The important thing is...oops." She'd dropped a card again. How very strange. Just one card. And she knew before she turned it over what it would be.

Yep. Her breath caught in her throat. Two swans, hearts, flowers, a pair of tiny kissing cupids flying in the air.

"The damn two of hearts," she muttered. This was getting ridiculous.

"What are you talking about?" he asked.

"The card, Jake. The card I keep pulling." She held it up to show him the picture. "The two of hearts."

"Fortune-telling cards?" He made a derisive snort. "You don't believe in that junk, do you?" His tone grew more mocking. "Don't tell me. It's magic. That's how you knew my name. You read it off one of your cards."

"Don't be absurd. I told you I saw it on your ID." She should've been insulted. But she decided not to be. Okay, so he was misguided and cynical. But he would learn. She had faith. She'd dealt herself the True Love card. She'd felt the connection between them. Didn't she feel this very minute that she could see right through him, clear to his heart?

Well, yeah, but...*yikes.* Even for her, this was taking a leap. He was self-righteous, he was way too honest, he had no apparent sense of humor, and he was...big. Very big.

Zoë chewed on a nail as she considered exactly what she was proposing. Nuttier than a fruitcake. Not likely to impress Jake.

But she was who she was. And Zoë Kidd was not afraid to take a risk. After all, how bad could it be? She'd expected to be going on this trip, anyway. In fact, she'd been looking forward to it. Meditation. Deep thinking. Personal growth. Surely she could do those things, make a break with the past, move on, and learn to be a better person, even if Jake was along. Even if he didn't seem likely to be cooperative.

She sent him a quick glance. Okay, so he clearly wasn't the meditation-and-deep-thoughts type. And he was more than a little intimidating, with that glower and the sizzle of sensuality she couldn't ignore.

"Oh, yeah. *That,*" she said under her breath. "If I went along, what would I do about that?"

"What did you say?"

But she didn't answer, still speculating on this wild idea. Could she really do this?

The eyes, the shoulders, the body that looked hard and hot in all the right places...and those lips. A girl could get lost in those lips for a long, long time. Could she *not* do this?

If he was intimidating, he was also yummy, no two ways about it. Yummy in a once-in-a-lifetime way. Although it seemed unlikely, he might just be her True Love. That idea made her stomach flutter again, but she squashed the fear. Maybe she wasn't considering this as a selfish path to True Love. Maybe it was because he was on some sort of mission that she could help with.

Good for her, good for him.

She could no longer ignore the fact that her intuition was pushing her in his direction. Hard.

She mashed together every ounce of courage she could muster. "How badly do you want to go on this trip?"

"I have to go," he said flatly. "Just name your price and I'll buy."

"But you only want one of my tickets." She moved closer, waving the two of hearts. "And what will I do with the other one?"

He shrugged. "If you'll only sell them together, then I'll buy both and toss one."

All in a rush, she said, "I'll let you buy Wylie's. But I'm keeping mine. I want to use it."

A half smile curved his adorable lips. "You want to use it, huh?" he asked dryly. "For what?"

Zoë smiled. The True Love card felt hot against her palms as she pressed it between both hands. "If you want to go, Jake, you'll need a partner. So I'm going with you."

3

JAKE LAUGHED. "Yeah, right. Like that's going to happen."

But the feisty little redhead wasn't giving in. He could tell that by the determined look on her face. Just his luck. He needed entry into this tour group, there was only one person with an entry pass available, and she turned out to be a Grade-A flake, doing some kind of goofy acrobatics half-dressed in a sweltering, unlocked apartment, burning a boatload of candles that smelled suspiciously like marijuana, waving fortune-telling cards around, and refusing to hand over her ticket to a trip she didn't want to make, anyway. And then there were her clothes.

Okay, at least he'd seen enough of her by now to be about ninety percent sure she wasn't "Toni," the object of his search. He'd checked out her feet and legs, and she didn't match. No toe rings, no sparkly sandals, plus her feet looked a lot smaller than the ones in the picture.

He'd checked out a lot more than her feet.

He'd walked in on a truly delectable view of her frisky little bottom pointed his way, and then she'd turned around and given him a gander at her front side, which made a wet–T-shirt contest look tame. He was a guy, okay? Maybe an in-control, by-the-book guy, but still a guy. When small, round, perfectly shaped breasts were presented right in front of him, covered only by one layer of slick, wet fabric, he couldn't look away. His mouth watered again just thinking about it.

She didn't seem to be at all aware that her clothing—or lack thereof—was downright provocative. She *did* seem to be aware that he was aware, however.

Or maybe it was just the ungodly temperature in the apartment making them both so hot and bothered. He ran a hand through his hair. He had no idea what was happening here, except that it was rapidly getting out of control. All he could think about was getting his hands on her tantalizing curves.

Time to stop that right then and there. Time to get back on track.

"I'll buy both tickets," he announced, reaching for his checkbook. This was on his father's tab, after all. What difference did it make how much he spent? And the sooner he disposed of this, the sooner he would be rid of Zoë Kidd.

"Oh, no, you won't!" she shot back with enough fire to make him want to spank her. Or kiss her. Or both. "I'll let you buy one. But you don't get to tell me what to do with my other ticket."

"Zoë, I—"

"Nope. Discussion over." He started to advance on her, but she held up a hand. "Don't think you can change my mind. If you want to go, it's my way or the highway."

"I hate it when people say that." Her way or the highway. He had six or seven inches and at least fifty pounds on her and she was bossing him around. But she had the ticket.

She crossed her arms over her breasts, thankfully blocking his view for a little while, and gave him the most bullheaded look he'd ever seen in his life. Consid-

ering the family he came from, that was saying something. "Here's the deal. We need to be at O'Hare by ten
in the morning. So you'll need to pick me up by eight,
just to be sure. Rush-hour traffic, you know." She
marched back over to her desk, rooting around for a second and coming up with an envelope with a big "EJ"—
Explorer's Journey—logo on the outside. "The instructions are in here about what to pack."

"Where exactly—" he began, but she cut him off,
yanking out a sheet of paper and handing it over.

"I'll give you the ticket and the rest of the details in the
morning. Oh, and be sure to leave the gun at home. They
won't let you keep it, anyway. Bad karma."

"It varies from state to state whether I could bring it,
and since I don't know where..." He gave her a wary
look, not at all liking how this was starting to sound. Did
she say *karma?*

This was not turning out well. There was something
very screwy about Zoë Kidd. Cute, pushy and screwy.
His least favorite kind of woman.

And he sure as heck didn't want to be stuck with her
all the way to wherever it was they were going. He sent
her one more glance, noting that she was smiling, which
was pretty frightening. Shaking his head, Jake turned to
leave.

"See you tomorrow, partner," she called out.

"We're not partners," he shot back. "We're going on
the same tour. But separately. Got it?"

She just kept beaming at him. "We can sort it out tomorrow."

Jake strode through the door without looking back.
Let her have her small victories tonight. Once she
handed over his ticket in the morning, there was nothing
she could do to him.

"If she insists on tagging along," he said under his breath, "it's not like we'll be attached at the hip. I'll stay as far away as possible."

"Don't be late!" she yelled behind him.

But he just shook his head and got out of there before Zoë Kidd did any more damage to his psyche.

JAKE WAS SOMEWHAT CHEERED up by the packing list. *Please leave valuable jewelry, watches, etc., at home. You won't need much in the way of clothing,* it continued, *since we provide all that for you. You may also choose one special item of personal significance, like a stuffed animal or a keepsake.* That struck him as fairly goofy, but even goofier was the fact that he already knew what Zoë would bring. It would definitely be that stupid tarot card she kept clutching last night, looking as if she was going to kiss it or cry over it.

As he put the last of his things in his duffel bag, Jake pressed his lips into a disapproving line. He'd busted a fortune-teller once. Some loser from the suburbs had paid big bucks to a self-proclaimed "mystic healer" in Old Town to get a curse lifted. And then, when the loser's luck at the track didn't change, the guy had proceeded back to Old Town to try to choke his money out of the mystic healer. After which said healer had cracked him over the head with her crystal ball. When Jake came in to break up the fight, the lady told him he was cursed now, too. Yeah, right. If Zoë was into that stuff, she was more seriously demented than he thought. Which was another reason to steer clear.

Hanging on firmly to that idea, he cast his mind over the packing list, one item at a time, as he drove up Lake Shore Drive, heading north to pick up Zoë. After all, he was a cop. He could look at evidence and draw conclusions, couldn't he?

First off, there had been nothing in the papers about passports or foreign currency, so they must be staying in the country at least. No hiking boots, no special equipment. And no mention of parkas or warm boots. So maybe it was somewhere warm.

"Let it be Palm Springs," he said as he pulled up in front of Zoë's building. "Or Hilton Head. Someplace with sand and ocean. A golf course. Scuba diving."

Of course, if he had his druthers, he would be headed to a plain old lake full of trout, with a fishing pole, some bait...and no Zoë.

He frowned. How had she described this trip? A honeymoon crossed with group therapy. Sounded ridiculous. Like Club Med for neurotic people who wanted to whine about their rotten childhoods in between cocktails, parasailing and heavy doses of honeymoon sex.

"Aw, jeez." That was one wrinkle he hadn't considered. Accommodations. He certainly had no intention of getting close enough to Zoë to have sex be any kind of a problem, but a honeymoon suite might be awkward. He could just see Zoë insisting they share the bed. *We won't touch*, she would say. *You paid half. It's only fair.*

Sharing a bed? With Zoë Kidd? Jake gritted his teeth.

Yeah, well, maybe the accommodations would be awkward, but not impossible. Surely he could sleep on the sofa for a few days. He had a momentary vision of Zoë traipsing around in her undies or her clingy, skimpy exercise wear, all wet with sweat...

Maybe he could sleep on the beach.

He smacked a hand into the steering wheel. Whatever it took, whatever the problems, he would get around them. Because he had no intention of sharing a room—or a bed—with Zoë Kidd.

He glanced up at her windows, on the second floor above a New Age shop that he seriously suspected of selling drug paraphernalia. "She's screwy all right. Living above a head shop and leaving her door wide-open."

Although he was prepared to go up to get her, he didn't need to. She ran out the minute he pulled up, and he decided he at least had to admire her enthusiasm, especially at this hour of the morning. It might be well before eight, but she was already perky and ready, wearing some kind of soft, low-rise pants that exposed her belly button, a white peasant top with embroidery on it, and flat shoes that made a flapping noise as she ran out to the car. Presentable. And a heck of a lot more clothes than last night, thank goodness. Plus there was the added grace that this morning she was dry. His body still wasn't recovered from the long, long cold shower he'd taken when he got home.

"Hi there," she said happily, dropping a small bag in the back seat of his old Ford and hopping into the front seat next to him.

"Have you got the tickets?" he asked.

"Don't waste time saying good-morning or anything."

"I won't."

"So you're not a morning person, is that it?" she said sympathetically.

Somebody honked at him, trying to get him to leave his parking space. He ignored it. "Do you have the tickets?" he asked again.

"Yes, sir," she answered smartly, making fun of him all the way. She dug into the goofy straw purse she was carrying and produced the same envelope he'd seen last night.

"I want mine now," he told her. "Hand it over."

"Nope. I can't. There's just one pass for both of us." She grinned, holding up a square yellow laminated card with "Your Ticket to Exploration" and "Couple Confirmed" stamped on it. "We have to enter the program two by two. Like Noah's ark."

This just kept getting worse and worse. As he pulled out into traffic and headed toward the expressway, he asked darkly, "They don't shackle us together or anything, do they?"

Her smile widened. "No, but they might if we asked nicely."

Jake groaned. Undertaking a ridiculous journey with a chirpy morning person was bad enough, but one with a body that wouldn't quit and a habit of sticking it way too close to him—and now, bringing up shackles, as in handcuffs, not the way he usually thought of them, on a perp headed for jail, but instead as something to do with brass beds and naughty games—it was a nightmare.

"I was kidding," she assured him, patting his hand where it lay on the steering wheel. He tamped down the impulse to jerk his hand away. She added casually, "I'm not into that kind of thing. I believe in free, unfettered sex where you can move around."

Which was way more information than he needed. *Way* more. "I want one thing clear," he announced. "We may be going in on the same pass, but we are going separately. There's you." With his left hand on one side of the wheel, he slid his right to the total opposite edge. "And then there's me. No *us*. Got it?"

She made some sort of noncommittal noise he took as a yes. Purposely not looking at her or her body, Jake tried to keep conversation to a minimum on the way to the airport. But damned if she didn't ask questions non-stop.

"So you're a cop. How long have you been doing that?" she opened with. "Do you like it?"

"Eight years. I like it fine." He kept his eyes on the car in front of him. Road repair. Traffic slow down. Not paying attention to Zoë. Not at all.

"And what do you do? Do you pound a beat?" she asked, scooting a little closer. "Is that what they call it?"

"A beat, yeah, some people call it that. But that's not what I do." He didn't even glance her way. "Put on your seat belt."

"All right, all right."

If she interrogated all the men she met this way, it was no wonder she was taking her honeymoon trip solo. Except she wasn't. *He* was there. Tortured, hog-tied, provoked...but he was along for the ride.

"So what do you do?" she prompted, safely fastening herself in. "Since you're not pounding a beat, I mean."

"I'm a sergeant," he said gruffly. "And a supervisor for tactical teams." He held up a hand. "And before you ask, tactical teams keep an eye on criminal activity in the district. Mostly undercover, looking for burglaries, gangs, narcotics, syndicates moving in, anything like that. We gather info, put two and two together, watch for patterns."

"Cool. And does this trip have something to do with your job?" she asked, turning practically sideways inside her shoulder harness so that she could look at him more directly. "This woman you're looking for, is she related to gangs or drugs or something?"

"No."

"Is she dangerous? Like, armed and dangerous? Maybe a fugitive from justice?"

He cracked a smile. "You've been watching too much TV."

"So is she a fugitive?"

"No," he allowed. "Not as far as I know." That was the truth, wasn't it?

"Good," she put in, relaxing into her seat. "I mean, I'm up for some excitement while we look for her, but nothing involving bodily harm."

"While *we* look for her? You're not looking. *I* am."

But she didn't react or respond to that observation. "You still haven't said what you want with her." She waited. "Well?"

He'd learned one thing over the years. Just because someone asked you a question didn't mean you had to answer it. He didn't.

"So you're not going to tell me?"

"Nope," he returned.

"Not even a hint?"

"Look, Zoë, this isn't a game," he said sharply. "It isn't a mission, it isn't a date, it isn't Twenty Questions, and I'm not going to tell you anything, so you might as well stop asking."

Okay, so he was being a little meaner than he ought to. He frowned, trying to decide whether he should be nicer, because, after all, he still needed that damn ticket. But then he hazarded a glance her way and caught the look on her face. What the...?

Her feelings weren't hurt. In fact, she looked...turned-on. *Oh, no.*

Curiosity sparkled in her pretty green eyes, and her expressive features were rapt with interest as she leaned his way. Big mistake. His close-mouthed approach had created a monster.

"Why are you looking at me like that?" he asked, as if he didn't know.

He could see the wheels turning, and the hint of color that tinged her cheeks. She started to answer, changed her mind, got even rosier and finally said, "I'm finding all this quite fascinating."

What was she talking about? Him? The hunt for Toni, which she wasn't even in on? "What exactly do you find fascinating?"

"Well, this trip. Yesterday I thought I would be bumming around, same old, same old, and today, here I am, on a trip into the unknown." She was positively beaming over there. "I'm stoked. How about you?"

"Not so much."

"Oh, come on. It will be great. Relaxing, you know."

Jake angled his chin to the side window. "Relaxing? Around you? I don't think so," he said under his breath.

But Zoë was moving on. Carefully she declared, "Jake, yesterday... I just feel it's only right to tell you. Yesterday, I felt some sort of heightened connection between us. I think you felt it, too." When he didn't respond, she prompted, "Yes?"

"No."

"Yes, you did."

He shouldn't have looked over at her, but it was too late now. She was smiling. You could say whatever you wanted, but there was no denying that Zoë had a spectacular smile, all bright and shiny, with just a hint of mischief. It mixed innocence and heat in a way he'd never really experienced, like she was the girl next door who would open that door and invite you in to play Strip Twister.

Yeah, Jake, great image. He needed to keep a wide berth between Zoë and any game where you ended up naked.

He glanced back at her. She was still smiling that saucy Strip-Twister smile. The girl was a menace.

And now she was on about some kind of connection between the two of them. What did she mean by that? The parlor trick of pulling his name out of thin air? Or the physical thing, where he kept drooling on her and she kept sniffing around him?

Jake figured the better part of valor was denial. "I did not feel any connection," he contended.

"Pooh."

"I've never met anyone who used the word 'pooh'."

Ignoring that comment, she hitched her legs up on the seat, which was tough to do inside the seat belt, but she seemed to be a very limber girl. *Bad thought, Jake. Don't go there.*

"So, Jake, tell me. Did you always know you wanted to be a policeman? Do you have to go to school for that?"

If he told her about his family and his training and all that boring stuff, at least it would keep her quiet and his mind busy the rest of the way to the airport. Talking about three generations of Calhouns in the Chicago Police Department was miles away from Strip Twister.

It wasn't until he parked his car in the lot at O'Hare that he realized how quickly the time had passed and how much he'd talked about himself. Who needed bright lights and rubber hoses? Zoë had just worked more out of him than most trained interviewers got out of suspects, especially closemouthed suspects like him, and she didn't even appear to be trying that hard. It was not a comforting thought.

"Which airline?" he asked, as they toted their bags and navigated their way to the terminal.

"None."

"None?" He held the elevator door for her. "What do you mean, none?"

"It's a bus," she said helpfully. "We leave from the bus terminal. It's in the instructions. There's supposed to be a red line on the floor and it goes right to the bus terminal."

"There was nothing about a bus in the instructions you gave me," he retorted. "Where the hell are we headed, anyway? Where can you get by bus?"

"Wisconsin."

"Wisconsin?" But that's where he was supposed to be right now, with his brothers, at the lake cabin. "Why can't we just drive ourselves?"

"It's all part of the program," she said patiently. "You're supposed to become a part of the group, plus you make a commitment for the whole deal. Like, once you get on that bus, there's no going back."

Just when he thought things were as bad as they could get, Zoë kept proving him wrong. "I was hoping for someplace a little more interesting, as long as I had to..."

Be on this idiotic tour. He didn't say that. But his visions of golf courses and scuba diving vanished. This sounded more like summer camp. They'd probably be tying knots and weaving flyswatters out of newspaper.

The rest of the way to the bus terminal, up escalators and down and around long corridors, she kept telling him not to be so grumpy and he kept wanting details she wasn't providing, while they both held their voices down so as not to attract too much attention from the people around them.

"Snap out of it, Jake. You're lucky you have me."

He wasn't feeling lucky. "Is there anything else you haven't told me?" he demanded. "Like the fact that this program you keep referring to is for recovering substance abusers or a bunch of mopes avoiding jail time by picking up litter in Wisconsin?"

"I told you, it's for newlyweds." Zoë rolled her eyes. "Quit being a cop for a minute, will you?"

"I'm not being a cop. You're being evasive," he contended. "You held back the bus info and the little detail that we were going to Wisconsin."

"You didn't tell me that our mode of transportation or the specific location made a difference to you," she said logically. "You were very adamant that you wanted to go on the Explorer's Journey and how or where didn't matter."

She was right. He hated that.

"And," she went on, "they don't provide a lot of details. It says right in the packing info, which I did give you, that they don't want you coming in with preconceived notions or preparing ahead. So they told us it's in Wisconsin, that we go on a bus, what to pack, and when we get there we'll be working on exercises involving serenity and trust and sharing and communication, stuff like that. That's pretty much it."

"Serenity? I've got plenty, thanks," he said with a certain edge. What a bunch of hooey.

"Yeah, well, I think you could use a little more." Zoë shook her head. "I think this program might be very good for you." When he didn't respond, she added, "Maybe it's your karma to be here for that very reason, you know, to work on serenity and trust and sharing, stuff like that."

"I don't think I have a karma." He held up his right hand. "And I don't think I want one."

"Your karma is going to bite you in the butt if you don't watch out," she said indignantly. "Besides, if you want to pass as a regular old person on the trip and find this woman, you're going to have to play along." Mocking his gesture earlier, she lifted both hands, leaving them about three feet apart, wagging one and then the other. "I know you're into this *me* over here and *you* over there and no *us* in between. But it's not going to work. Look around you. Look at the other people on the tour. Do you want to fit in or not?"

She pointed to a cluster of people standing under a bright yellow banner with a big EJ logo and then Explorer's Journey printed under it. Outside the glass doors, he could see the bus waiting there. It, too, was yellow, with the same intertwined *E* and *J* logo splashed across the side.

Jake slowed. Damn it, she was right. He *was* lucky she was with him. Without her, he would've stood out like a sore thumb. The other tour goers were milling around, mostly not in line yet, but they were still all two by two, arm in arm, some kissing and canoodling, and a few even fighting. One pair seemed to be doing both at the same time. These people were attached at the hip. A man by himself would've been anything but undercover.

"Are you convinced?" Zoë asked. "Ready to be partners?"

Not on your life. But he nodded, trying to figure out a way to make this work, as Zoë took his hand and dragged him along.

It couldn't be that hard, could it? After all, he'd lain in alleys pretending to be unconscious while drug deals went on over his head and he'd gone undercover as a potential john in massage parlors and strip joints. Standing next to Zoë and acting like one half of a couple for five minutes should be a piece of cake. Okay, so she was feisty and weird and unpredictable. He'd dealt with worse and come out alive. He frowned. No way he couldn't take on Zoë.

As they walked around to get in line, Jake surveyed the prospects, mindful of his real purpose, which was finding Toni the blackmailer. But there were two or three women of her approximate height and shape judging from Vince's fuzzy photos, and no one in the sparkly high heels that would've been a dead giveaway.

"Do you see her?" Zoë whispered, her eyes wide.

"Shh." He draped an arm around her, guiding her into a place in line.

But Zoë wasn't through. "There are only four couples ahead of us. That means most everyone will be behind us, so keep an eye out," she warned, cocking her head in the direction where already three more couples had fallen into place. "If we spot her now, we can try to sit by her on the bus and eavesdrop."

Little Miss Detective had to be nipped in the bud before she made a hash of things. Leaning down, he got right next to her ear, figuring everyone else would think it was some kind of sweet talk. Too bad he had to notice what a nice ear she had, all pink and little, with a nice soft lobe he had the urge to bite. Damn it, anyway.

"Listen, Zoë," he muttered, "you are not helping me, okay? I'm playing along with hanging out together, like a twosome, to blend in. But this is not a partnership. So just be quiet and stay out of the way."

"That's not going to work," she began, but her words were drowned out by a reed-thin blond woman in a tracksuit standing directly under the yellow banner. She was carrying a clipboard and waving her arms.

"People!" she called out. "I'm Sandra, your tour director for this first leg. Welcome!" She paused long enough to smile broadly. "It looks like almost everyone is here," she went on, "and we'll be loading the bus soon. We will check your names against our master list, so please get into the line now, and have ID ready. And then we have a photographer right outside the door to take photos of each couple. After you have your picture taken, please get right on the bus. We want to do this as quickly as we can so that we can get underway, bringing you that much closer to your magical journey of exploration."

"Magical journey of exploration?" Jake asked, raising an eyebrow. If they spread any more manure around, he was going to need a shovel.

"You'd better not—" Zoë began, but he cut her off.

"Yeah, yeah, I know. I'm good. I'm blending."

The first and then the second couple checked in and moved out the door toward the photographer and the bus. Jake tightened his arm around Zoë, keeping her firmly faced forward so she couldn't do any obvious snooping. Meanwhile, he did case the line up and down over her head. A couple more maybes, but nothing that really struck him. Finally it was their turn at the front of the line.

"Zoë Kidd," she said to the woman with the clipboard, offering up her driver's license and the yellow confirmation card.

The blonde took the card, gave Zoë back her license, then grinned at Jake. "You must be Wylie. ID, please?"

"Uh, no," Zoë interceded. "I actually dumped Wylie and went with Jake instead. Much better choice."

The tour director scowled.

Zoë joked, "I traded up." No comment from the woman in charge. "Well, you know, considering we got married on the fly, I guess we *really* need the program now."

The woman shook her head as she looked down at her list, but she put a dark slash through Wylie's name. "So if you're not Wylie, you are...?" she asked crisply.

"Jake," he said as quietly as possible, handing over his driver's license.

"You should have given us more notice that you were switching husbands," the blonde noted in a rather peeved tone. "Jake Calhoun," she read aloud off the license, penciling it in on her list. "Well, Mr. Calhoun, your documents are going to be wrong all week."

Her voice was louder than he really appreciated. If Toni was anywhere near and heard the name Calhoun, it might warn her off.

The woman continued to fuss as she pulled the name tag out of his badge, flipped it over, and wrote "Jake" in big, fat letters. "And without his name ahead of time, we didn't do the usual background checks. We like to know who's coming, you see, because we believe the Explorer's Journey is a very special and select program and we want to insure the safety of all of our guests."

"It's okay," Zoë put in. "He's a cop. Show her your badge, Jake. He's good to go."

"Um, Zoë, let's not go there," he said in a low tone. To the thin blonde, he asked, "Do you have any kind of roster of the tour that you can hand out?"

"Why would you need that?"

"Just to know who we're traveling with," he said with a shrug. "I like to know people's names."

"They're on the name tags—" she began, but was distracted by a sudden ruckus that developed near the end of the line.

Damn it. Jake wanted that roster to get a head start on

who the possibilities might be, based on names. But Sandra wasn't paying attention.

Although his view was obstructed by the disarray of honeymoon couples and their bags, by force of habit, he shifted to get a better angle, wondering what the deal was back there. He saw a man with a sleeveless T-shirt and tattoos, slumped and glum, opposite his wife, who was shouting on and on about something. She was a lot shorter than the guy, plus other people were clustering around, so Jake's view was mostly blocked, although he could hear the shrill voice, see waving arms and make out a frizzy brown ponytail that bobbed up and down. Marital dispute. Nothing too dramatic. Nothing Jake needed to get involved with and blow his cover so quickly.

Still, Sandra the tour director seemed to be quite concerned that an unhappy couple might spoil the mood for everyone else. Spinning back to Jake and Zoë and quickly handing back his license, she dumped the pair of name tags in Zoë's hands and said hastily, "You're fine. You two go ahead. Don't hold up the line." Giving them a small push toward the door, she sprinted off toward the trouble spot.

As Zoë craned her neck, Jake caught her hand and gave her a swift tug out the door toward the photographer. "Let's get this moving, okay? The sooner we get to Wisconsin and get this started, the better."

Zoë peered behind them. "I wonder what that was all about. The fight, I mean."

"Why are you so interested?"

"I'm just trying to be attentive," she contended. "You know, be a good observer and witness."

That was all he needed. "Will you stop with the detective work, already? It doesn't concern you. You're not helping."

That got Zoë's attention. She fixed him with a no-nonsense stare that would've done his father proud. Very softly but firmly, she said, "Oh, yes, I am. You said your mystery woman would be on this tour. Do you want to find her or not?"

Jake had no answer to that. Damn it. How was he going to get Zoë off the scent and out of his way?

"Come on, you two, closer," the photographer coaxed, tugging them along the sidewalk and up against a cardboard cutout with the name of the tour swirling over their heads. He consulted a list. "Put your arm around her, Wylie."

"Jake," he corrected.

He couldn't help it. She was right there, looking up at him, and the photographer had ordered him to get closer. And she really was an infuriating woman. If she wanted to play footsie with him, maybe he would just illustrate the danger of her position. So he slid an arm around her waist and yanked her up against him, smiling when she made a little yelp.

"How about a kiss?" The man held up the camera. "Remember, it's your honeymoon, kids. Make it good. On the count of three..."

Pulling her completely into his arms, Jake leaned in, staring down into her eyes. The sparkle of mischief was still there, but her gaze was wide and a little wary.

The photographer said, "One..."

Her lips parted. "Jake, I don't think—"

He didn't even wait to hear the *two*, let alone the *three*. Frustration, annoyance and a whole lot of heat unspooled inside him, as Jake bent nearer. Cutting off her words completely, he covered her mouth with his.

4

DIZZY. DRIFTING. Seeing stars.

Was she still standing? Zoë wasn't sure. His mouth was so warm and soft and sure, downright intoxicating, as he plunged deeper one second and then nipped her the next, confusing her, overwhelming her, making her want to slide right in and stay awhile. Irresistible.

She made a little yelp of pleasure into his mouth as she hung on, wrapping her arms tighter around his neck, pressing up into him, wanting this moment to last forever. Insanity.

Somewhere in the periphery of her vision, there were a couple of loud clicks and someone said, "Okay, that's good. You can stop now."

But Jake didn't stop. And Zoë didn't, either. Hungry for more, she closed her eyes and went for it. She started to nibble him back, tipping her head to the side, tugging him down, splaying her fingers through the soft strands of hair at the back of his neck. Luscious.

"Excuse me." There was someone tapping on her shoulder. "You have to get on the bus now."

She paid no attention.

"Move along!" the man said more loudly. "The line's backing up. Plenty of time for that once you get there."

Jake broke from the kiss, firmly setting her down about a foot away from him.

Zoë glanced up at him in confusion. What the hell had

just happened here? He looked about as blown away as she felt, but she could see him recover his senses first, as his jaw clenched and that familiar guarded expression returned.

She fingered her bruised and cut lower lip. Had he really bitten her? Or had she bitten him? How savage. How wild. *How amazing.*

It was one thing to be attracted to him and think, *Gee, maybe, you know, in the abstract, he could be my true love. Maybe I'll ride along on this trip and see if I like him.* It was quite another to lose control completely.

She had never behaved that way in her life. "But *he* kissed *me*," she whispered, shaking her head. Which made it even worse.

He was the one who kept insisting they weren't a team, not together, just two individuals. He absolutely denied any connection between them, and *he* kissed *her.* And not a little peck between pals, either. This was an all-out, down-and-dirty smoochfest. This was lust and love and war, all mashed together into one relentless kiss.

"What was that for?" she demanded, as he picked up both bags and tossed them into the luggage compartment.

"We can talk about it later," he said under his breath.

"When?"

"Later," he repeated. He practically hauled her up into the bus and down the middle, waiting for her to jump into a window seat and then cutting her off by taking the aisle.

There wasn't a whole lot of room in the seats, and Jake was a larger-than-average man, meaning he was pretty well crammed into his seat, but somehow he managed to hold himself over there far enough not to be touching her anywhere from stem to stern. Zoë stared at his rigid profile, her eyes lingering on his lips. Oh, those lips. Those delicious, devastating lips.

What did he think he was doing, kissing her like that? She couldn't stand the idea of making it one mile closer to Wisconsin without sorting it out.

"Well?" she said, keeping her voice very low as the bus got underway.

Jake kept his focus straight ahead. "Well what?"

"About the kiss."

"What about it?"

Zoë tried to keep it quiet, but it was tough with all the suppressed energy threading through her. She had to sit on her hands to stop herself from waving them in the air in pure frustration. "It was unbelievable. It was more than unbelievable. If I hadn't already thought there was this, you know, zam-sizzle-boom thing going on between us, I sure would have known after that kiss."

"Zam, sizzle, boom, huh?" he echoed.

Studiously ignoring her, Jake seemed to make a show of scanning the seats on the bus. He even pulled a notebook and pen out of his pocket and wrote a few things down. Mr. Avoidance, she thought angrily.

Peering over his shoulder, she could see he'd made a neat grid, with hair colors and body types cross-referenced with little check marks. How very nice. He was in investigation mode while she could still feel the impression of his lips on hers, the aftershocks where his tongue had slipped deep into her mouth.

His tongue... *Stop thinking about that. Now.*

She put a hand on his arm, stilling his pen. "You kissed me, bucko. So stop denying the chemistry."

"I'm not," he protested.

At least he was looking her in the eye. She could feel

her hand tingle where it lay on his shirtsleeve, adding more proof to her chemistry theory. She snatched it back.

"Yeah, you're right. It was an incredible kiss," he admitted, looking tense and annoyed. "And I'm sorry, okay? Bad move. The guy told me to kiss you and I did. Spur of the moment. It was a mistake. Spur-of-the moment things usually are."

"No, they're not," she said slowly, but he clearly wasn't listening.

"It was a miscalculation," he went on. "We were thrown together, and it happened. But that's all it was. Lots of strangers share knock-your-socks-off kisses. It's part of life."

"It is?" She narrowed her eyes at him. "On what planet? 'Cause I think I want to move there."

He went back to his notebook, apparently making notes about his fellow passengers, squinting at various rows. "I'm sorry, Zoë. My mistake. But don't worry. It's not going to happen again."

"Why not?" Her annoyance level was rising. It was one thing for *her* to think it was risky and try to proceed more slowly. But it was quite another for him to kiss her like that and then completely withdraw the prospect of it happening again. They could at least test it. Would they get the same explosive chemical reaction? Or would trying a few more kisses add up to a total fizzle? Surely it was her duty to find out.

She hitched up far enough in her seat to look over into the next few rows. "Pretty much everyone is making out around here. If we want to pass as a couple of newly-weds, we might as well get with the program." She eyed his mouth hungrily. "I'm willing to take a few kisses for the good of the show if you are."

"Okay, wait a minute." He yanked her back down into her seat. "I thought if I proved to you what a dangerous game you were playing, you would back off. Damn you, anyway, you keep doing exactly the opposite of what I expect."

Zoë tried to process that. "So you kissed me hoping to scare me off?"

Silence.

"That was a really stupid idea, Jake. Which is exactly why you need me helping you. Come on. Admit it." Zoë poked him. "You liked it. The kiss, I mean. You liked it a lot. Well, surprise! So did I. Just proves even more what a good idea it was to do this together."

Jake shook his head. "We can't. *You* can't. The idea was to lay low, under the radar, cool and calm and keeping an eye on everyone else. But I never said I was going to actively attempt to play a newlywed."

"We have to blend in," she argued. "C'mon, work with me here. I'm trying. You're not. And it's your mission, not mine. Well, sort of. I mean, it's mine now, too. But you're the one with the most at stake."

She knew that was a lie the minute she said it. Somehow, some way, she seemed to have quite a bit riding on this little excursion, too. She'd known that the minute she pulled the True Love card. Well, she'd hoped. And then when he kissed her, it felt like...

Zoë swallowed, looking away from him. It felt like *forever*. And it was way too early for that. Especially with someone as prickly and downright irritating as Jake Calhoun. She sent her gaze back his way, trying to stop all the weird flipping and flopping happening in her stomach every time she so much as glanced at him. *Good God.* If she felt this attached after one kiss, how would she react if she *slept* with him?

The flipping escalated into a whole gymnastics routine with that idea. Okay, better back up slowly and never think about it again. Way too dangerous.

True to form, Jake just continued to glower at her.

As calmly as she could manage, Zoë said, "It doesn't much matter what we do. Everyone's going to think we're newlyweds, anyway."

He dropped any pretense of working with his notebook, shoving it back into his jacket pocket. "And by acting like newlyweds, you mean hanging all over each other?"

More kisses like the last one? Zoë slid her tongue over the bite mark in her lip. So much for avoiding the danger of being close to Jake. "I'm game," she offered.

"Well, I'm not. And I can't believe you are," he argued, looking at her as if she had some dread disease. "You come along on something that you don't know anything about, with a guy that you don't know anything about. On the rebound. What about this Wylie guy?"

With a small sigh, Zoë unhooked both braids pinned to the top of her head and started to thread her fingers through her hair and massage her scalp. Maybe her braids were too tight. Maybe that's why she couldn't think straight.

"What about him?" he persisted. "You know, the guy you were going to marry?"

Zoë kept her mouth shut.

"As I recall, you were planning to marry him within the fairly recent past. Doesn't it seem strange to be taking off on a trip with some new guy right after losing the last fiancé?"

"If I'm not concerned, why should you be?" she inquired coolly, tossing her hair.

"Zoë, did you ever think maybe this is a rebound thing for you?" He stopped. He had the oddest expression on his face. "What are you doing to your hair?"

"I, uh, just thought I would let it down. Why, does it look weird?"

Feeling self-conscious, she fluffed it, letting the red waves settle around her face. It was getting long. She'd always worn it short, but in preparation for the wedding, she'd grown it out. But then she'd started wearing it up just to keep it out of the way, more often than not splitting it into two braids and fastening them over the top, just because it was easy. Now it felt strange floating to her shoulders.

"No, it's just..." He pressed his lips into a kind of grimace. "It's very pretty. Kind of soft. And the red...it's a, uh, nice color."

"Um, thank you." Just when she got used to dealing with grumpy Jake the quintessential just-the-facts-ma'am cop, he turned into sweet, irresistible Jake again, the one with the vulnerable blue eyes and the kissable mouth. She wanted him to kiss her so badly her mouth was watering.

It took him a second to regain his bearings. He pulled his gaze away from her hair and focused squarely on her face. "You didn't answer my question about the rebound thing."

"I am not on the rebound," she returned. How ridiculous. As if anyone would rebound from a loser like Wylie to a fabulous guy like Jake and spend two minutes worrying about it. "Satisfied?"

"Not hardly," he muttered, but she heard it, anyway.

Yeah, well, me neither, bucko. It's going to take more than one sensational kiss to satisfy me now.

She tried not to wiggle in her seat at the very idea of

satisfying and being satisfied by Jake. Why was it that everything acquired such a heightened sexual context in his presence?

But she took a different tack when she spoke aloud. "We're here, we're going to be there in a few hours, and it's too late to back out now," she told him. "So stop worrying. Blend."

"Blend, huh? You're really ready to just run off with me, kiss me, be with me, whatever, like it's nothing?" he challenged. "Even though this was going to be your honeymoon with him?"

"Okay, let's get this straight." Even though she had no desire whatsoever to keep putting Wylie in between them, even though Wylie was the last thing she was thinking about right now, she decided she was going to have to be forthright. Damn it. Keeping her gaze level and her voice low, she spelled it out for him. "I dumped him. He was very immature. He treated me like..." *Like I didn't count.* But she couldn't say that to Jake. "He didn't treat me very well, okay? When it came right down to it, there was no way I was going to marry someone like that." She knew she sounded angry, but she couldn't stop herself. "At least I figured out in time to get rid of him before I was tied to him for life. So I am not on the rebound. Have you got that now?"

"Yeah."

"Thank goodness." She slumped back in her seat, wondering what Jake would do if she screamed with frustration. How was it possible for one man to make her want to kiss him so badly and yet strangle him at the same time? "Please don't bring up Wylie again, okay? It makes me feel like a total loser."

"This isn't about him. It's about you," he said, and there was this kindness, this concern in his voice that made her feel even crankier. "Do you really know what you're doing? Have you thought about the ramifications of this?"

Well, no, she hadn't. "What ramifications?"

He shrugged, but his eyes were intent. "Like, what about sleeping arrangements? I was assuming we'd be in a hotel and an extra room would be no biggie. But now...some newlywed boot camp in Wisconsin? For all we know, they're going to throw us both in a tent with one sleeping bag. "

Sleeping arrangements. Well, he was right. That hadn't occurred to her. Although now that he'd mentioned it, ideas about Jake and the darkness and what trouble they could get up to during the long hours of night started running through her mind in all kinds of permutations and combinations. Really delicious ideas. Zoë held her breath for a second, unable to dismiss the images of tangled limbs and bare skin, lit only by moonlight.

Was she going to faint, right there on the bus? She exerted firm control, breathed in and out, and brought herself back to the real world and the real man.

After all, no matter what she might want to do with Jake in a big old honeymoon bed, there was no way he would let anything happen. She knew him. Jake would make sure it was all above board and squeaky clean. He would save her from her own lack of control. Wouldn't he?

Out loud, she said, "We'll deal with that when we get there. There's really no point in worrying about it now."

"I don't get you," he said in a certain aggrieved tone. "In my world, the women are the ones who get anxious about possibly sharing sleeping quarters with strange men. Not that I'm anyone to worry about. But you don't know that." Drawing his brows together, he declared, "You don't even know me."

"Oh, come on, Jake." She almost rolled her eyes again before she caught herself.

Yes, she had a few fears about Jake. Actually, it was more that she had fears for herself around Jake, that she wouldn't be able to control these crazy feelings that kept pushing her toward him. Or maybe she was just afraid she had made a very stupid mistake coming on this trip. Maybe she would lose her heart to him while he would never return those feelings and she would feel like a total idiot when all was said and done. But not because of who he was. Who he was was...upright. Foursquare. True blue.

She was perfectly safe with Jake. Which in some ways was a real shame.

Zoë gave him a small smile. "You are so obviously one of the good guys. I can read you like a book."

"Please don't tell me this is some psychic vision or something," he said caustically. "I saw you with those cards. Let me guess—as soon as I left last night, you whipped out the crystal ball and the tea leaves and they threw you a message from the great beyond, just to let you know I was a good guy."

Zoë blinked. "I—I don't have a crystal ball and I don't read tea leaves. I never said I was psychic." Which was clearly a good thing, considering the acid in his voice when he'd said the word. She guessed she'd better not tell him her theory about him and the True Love card. "I'm just a good judge of people," she contended. "A very good judge."

"Yeah, right. Which is why you were engaged to a loser and called it off at the eleventh hour."

Zoë couldn't keep her voice from rising. "I told you not to bring that up again!"

The woman across the aisle, a thirty-something whose husband was asleep, started to giggle and kind of snort, tipping herself far enough across to punch Jake in the shoulder. "You can sure tell you two aren't newly-weds."

Outed already. Immediately Zoë zipped her lip. So much for her theory that everyone would assume they were honeymooners and go with the flow.

"Yep," the lady went on. "Bickering like that—you must've been married awhile."

Zoë sagged with relief as the woman chortled again. "I've been married before, so I recognize the symptoms. What is it? Six, seven years? Getting that seven-year itch?"

Jake looked at Zoë and she looked at him, and they both knew which one would come up with a cover story on the fly.

"Actually, we *are* newlyweds," Zoë began in a confidential tone as she leaned over him to talk to the lady. He sat very still, and there was a little twitch in his cheek. Poor Jake. Truth tellers had such a hard time in the world.

She patted his thigh, trying to look like a newlywed, almost snatching her hand away when she felt his hard muscles clench under the denim. But she didn't. She left it right there to torture him. In fact, she fingered the fabric more closely, enjoying the play of sinew under there. She had to make it look good, didn't she?

Feeling naughty, she dipped her fingers lower, loving the way the blue of his eyes darkened as her thumb ran along his inseam. Under her hand, she could feel the heat emanating from his jeans. Whoa.

"Zoë," Jake warned in an undertone, directed so only she could hear it.

He looked ready to kill her, while she was ready to jump over into his side of the seat and have her way with him. *You are playing with fire, Zoë,* her conscience told her. *No,* she told it right back, *I'm playing with Jake...*

"You're not fooling me," the woman interjected, teetering out into the aisle, shoving her head even closer, pulling Zoë reluctantly back to the conversation. "You two are no newlyweds. I'm never wrong about these things."

"Oh, we're newlyweds all right. This time." Zoë smiled, trying to decide where to go with this little piece of fiction. How far could she push him before he cried uncle? Improvising as she went along, she deliberately twirled her fingers against his thigh as she announced, "This is our second go-around. Jake and I were married before when we were very young. So in love. Just *desperately* in love."

He muttered something under his breath that sounded like a curse. A bad one.

Zoë was loving this new feeling of power. Teasing Jake was an awful lot of fun. "Long story short—even though we were mad for each other, it was all passion and no foundation. Like, incredible flames but no wood underneath, you know?"

Jake choked when she said the word "wood," but maybe that was because she'd moved her thumb higher on his inseam. The lady across the aisle nodded, rapt.

"So even though there was this incredible, *incredible* heat between us, it didn't work out." She chuckled, lowering her voice. "Because you have to get out of bed sometime, you know?"

"Oh, I know!" the woman hastened to agree.

Jake groaned, placing his hand firmly over hers, removing it from his inseam, sticking it back on her side of the seat divide.

Figuring she had pushed him about as far as she could, Zoë finished up quickly. "So we married young, grand flame of passion, yadda yadda yadda, didn't work out, broke up, and then, just when I was going to marry someone else, Jake came back into my life at the absolute last moment and swept me off my feet. Again! Can you believe it?"

Looking grim, Jake whispered, "Don't make up anything you won't remember later."

As their new friend across the aisle made little oohs and aahs over the story, Zoë added, "So here we are, back again. Just can't stay away from each other." She reached over and pinched his cheek. "You better treat me right this time, mister."

"You two certainly do seem in love. Even the arguing." She added coyly, "And I can feel the heat from here."

"Sweet pea," Zoë cooed at Jake, pooching her lips and making smooching noises at him. She leaned in as close as she could get without actually touching his lips. Which was very close. Barely whispering, she murmured, "Aren't you adorable?"

The sad thing was, she really meant it.

"Okay, enough," he said darkly, grasping both her wrists tightly and fending her off. "You stop this right now or I'll stop the bus."

"Just trying to make it look good," she whispered.

As the husband across the aisle interrupted, telling his wife in no uncertain terms to be quiet so he could sleep, Zoë decided she should probably stop tormenting Jake. She might feel perfectly certain she knew who and what he was, but she didn't have a good grasp of his limits yet. Might as well not push her luck this early in the game.

She sighed and removed both her hands, sagged back into her seat and stared into the headrest of the person in front of her. What the heck was she doing? Teasing him, touching him, rubbing his inseam, threatening to kiss him. Wicked games.

But her resolve to back off and leave him alone lasted about three seconds. She turned to face him again. "You know, if we agree on how to go about this, set down some ground rules for this partnership, I won't have to improvise anymore. That might be a good thing, don't you think?"

Deadpan, not looking at her, he mumbled, "By all means, let's have rules. You and the seat of your pants make for a dangerous combo."

"Good. So we can shake on it. That we're going to be partners, I mean." She waited. She already knew that Jake was a man of his word. And if she made him come right out and make a pact, he wouldn't go back on it. "So, are we agreed? We're blending, we're partners, we're pretending to be newlyweds just like all the other newlyweds."

"I said okay."

She chewed her lip. "Do you mean it?"

Jake shifted in his seat enough to glare at her. "Zoë, you win. I have seen the wisdom of taking you on as a teammate, because I am damn sure not enjoying you as my adversary."

"Good. I think." She glanced down at the notebook still peeking out of his jacket pocket. "Okay, so do you want to write the rules down in your notebook?"

Casting a jaded eye her direction, he pulled it out of

his pocket and opened it up. "Number one," he said slowly, putting pen to paper. "No touching."

"Well, that's silly. We have to touch. We're newly-weds," she scoffed.

"Okay. Minimal touching." He sent a mocking glance her way. "And you have to keep your paws off anything below the waist. Like my pants."

Zoë licked her lips. And she had so enjoyed his inseam. "Touching as necessary to maintain the newly-wed image," she countered.

"Done. But no touching in private. And no sharing of sleeping quarters."

She considered it. "Okay. But you have to promise to tell me more about what you're doing, and to be a good sport about the exercises they give us."

"What exercises? What does that mean?"

"Well, I saw it on *Oprah*, and I can pretty much guarantee they're going to ask us to, oh, I don't know, meditate and lead each other around blindfolded and feed each other grapes." She paused. "Things you aren't going to like."

Jake closed his eyes. He took a deep breath.

Zoë waited for the other shoe to drop. "If we're going to pass, we're going to have to play along with the program and the exercises."

Finally he said, "And what are you asking me to promise with regard to these activities?"

He sounded so clipped and precise, so much like a cop, it made her want to run her fingers up his inseam again, just to get him to relax. She refrained. "I want you to promise you'll try. When they tell us to do stuff you think is stupid, you need to try. Can you do that?"

"Yeah," he said with another sigh. "I can try."

"Okay. I'm good." She sat up, feeling much happier.

She dropped her voice even lower. "And what about the investigation? You know, the mission?"

"What about it?" he asked slowly.

"What's my part?"

"None," he said flatly. "You don't have a part."

"But I can help," she told him in her most persuasive tone. "I told you, I'm a very good judge of character. You have to admit—two heads are better than one."

"Not always."

Zoë waited. "Jake, you know this isn't going to work if you're off spying on people or whatever it is you plan to do, and your new wife isn't by your side. Right?"

He ran a hand through the soft brown spikes of his hair. "This is my investigation," he said after a moment. "You can participate to the degree I think is wise. No more. Got it?"

"Uh-huh." *He's letting me in.* She felt triumphant.

"No arguments?"

"I never argue," she said sweetly.

"Yeah, right."

But she didn't care what he said at that point. For better, for worse, whether he liked it or not...

He was letting her in.

5

"WHATEVER YOU SAY, Jake," Zoë told him quickly. "This is your mission, and you're in charge."

"There is information I am not going to share with you, no matter what you do to me. So if I say it's private, it's private. Okay?"

"Sure." She smiled encouragingly. "Can you tell me what's in the notebook?"

"Just keeping track."

"Of who's who?" When he nodded, she added, "Got any suspects yet? There's a blonde in the fourth row who looks phony to me."

Jake raised an eyebrow, edging out into the open area far enough to see who she was talking about. "I hate to ask, but why do you think she looks phony?"

Matter-of-factly, hoping to prove herself by demonstrating good observation skills, she said, "Hair color from a box. Boobs way bigger and perkier than nature intended. A rock on her hand the size of Gibraltar. Total fake."

"You didn't see her shoes, did you?"

"Her shoes?" Every time she thought she had a handle on him, he threw another curve. Jake sure didn't seem like the type to care about shoes. "Why? You have a hankering for a woman in Manolo Blahniks?"

"I don't even know what that is. No, the woman I'm looking for wears see-through sandals. Bigger feet than you. High heels. Glittery. Straps crisscrossed around the ankle," he told her. "Plus lots of toe rings and nail polish."

She stared at him for a long moment. "You said this was private. But it better have no relation to anything remotely romantic, even in your past. Because she sounds like a hooker."

"If it was romantic, wouldn't I already know what she looks like?" he asked dryly.

"Maybe." She considered the possibilities, and her imagination quickly ran away with her. Beauty and the beast stories were always like this, where somebody didn't know what his lover really looked like. Beauty and the beast and hard-core porn. *Eeeeuw.* "I'm starting to wonder about blindfolds and dark closets and voyeurs with foot fetishes for women with toe rings and trashy plastic shoes. And I'm really grossing myself out here, so anytime you want to jump in..."

Jake laughed out loud. It was the first time she'd heard him laugh like that, free and unforced, and it sounded wonderful. "Voyeurs and foot fetishes? The way your mind works...Zoë, Zoë. What am I going to do with you? No, it's nothing romantic," he assured her. "The shoes and feet are all the info I have to go on. Medium height, medium build. That and the fact that she was blond the last time she was spotted. But that's easy enough to change. Although I don't think she knows anyone is on to her, so there's no real reason to change."

"Hmm..." She was feeling all intrigued and fascinated again. "I'm wondering why that is. About the only evidence you have being feet evidence, I mean. Very curious."

Jake didn't say anything, just kind of lowered his gaze and gave her that look again.

"Well, I haven't noticed any shoes like that on anyone on this trip." But even as she said the words, she had the weirdest glimmer of a thought, that maybe she *had* seen a pair of cheap, sparkly plastic sandals today. Had she? As quickly as it was there, the thought disappeared. "But I wasn't really looking before this. I will now, though," she promised. "Once we get off the bus."

"No, don't. I shouldn't have said anything. Forget it."

Darn. He let something fun slip and then he clammed up again. "I really can help look for shoes. That's an easy one, Jake. Probably easier for me than you, don't you think?"

"No," he said firmly. And then he put the notebook away, closed his eyes and leaned back in his chair, as if to broadcast the fact that he didn't want to talk about it.

"No fair not sharing," she grumbled. "One more reason you may just reap big benefits from the Explorer program when you are shown the error of your non-sharing ways. There is no *I* in team, you know."

But he didn't say anything. Either he was sleeping or he was doing a good imitation. She watched him for a while, feeling too wound up and unsettled to nap herself. Maybe if she jostled him he would wake up and she could make him talk. But he looked awfully sweet sleeping. It seemed a shame to disturb him, even if he was the most irritating and secretive man on God's green earth.

So she, too, settled in, turning away from him and toward the window, leaning her forehead against the back of her seat, watching a blur of rolling green hills and black-and-white cows flow by. She let her head slide away from the window, cushioned by the back of her seat, and she listened to the steady rhythm of Jake's breathing. In and out.

The rumble of the bus, the placid scenery, the warmth emanating from Jake...very soothing.

Zoë felt her eyelids growing heavy.

"WE'RE ALMOST HERE, everyone!" a jolly voice called out from the front of the bus. "If you could just gather your belongings, we'll be disembarking in a few minutes."

"Mmph?" Zoë was a light sleeper, but her eyes felt all gluey and stuck shut. And her body was crunched into the weirdest position. Where was she? What was under her cheek? Whose shoulder was that? And whose lap was she draped across? Whoever he was, he was warm and hard and solid. Edging her head to the side, she tilted back far enough to see his face. "Nice face," she murmured, taking it in in bits and pieces.

Clean jawline. Blue eyes. Very blue. Quirky lips, kind of narrow and clever, fuller on the bottom. She liked the look of those lips. A lot. What a good dream. Sliding one hand behind his neck, she tipped herself upward, hoping to be kissed.

Except she realized suddenly that she already had been intimate with that mouth. For real. And it was *good*.

Horrified, she jerked awake the rest of the way. "Jake?"

"Yeah." His voice sounded drowsy and indistinct. "We're here, wherever here is."

"But I'm..." In his lap? How did that happen?

She pitched herself upright, falling back against the window and nearly cracking her head. But Jake caught her by the hand and hauled her back in his direction. "Hold on. What's wrong with you?"

She could feel her cheeks flame. "I'm just kind of..." Awkwardly she maneuvered her legs back in her own seat and pretended to adjust her clothes.

"Oh. You were in my..." Jake sat up a little straighter, too. "Sorry."

"Yeah, me, too," she said quickly. "I don't know how I got there. I woke up kind of unexpectedly. I mean, I fell asleep unexpectedly. I don't usually take naps this time of day." She tried to stop the chatterbox routine before she did anything even more embarrassing. "Must have been the motion. Of the bus, I mean. I can't believe I fell asleep. On you. How...odd. Well, I guess we're one step ahead on the trust exercises, aren't we?" When he didn't say anything, she added lamely, "Trust. You know, because I trusted you enough to sort of fall asleep on you."

"Yeah," he said dryly. "I got it."

Yawning, she purposefully put herself all the way back in her own seat, turned away from him, and attempted a stretch in these cramped quarters. It didn't work. If she went backward, she would be in his lap again. So she peeked out the window. "It looks pretty nice. Can you see? There's a stone fence. And we're just pulling through a gate. Yikes. Electric."

Jake stayed where he was. "Looks like a prison."

"It does not. There are flowers and trees. And look, you can see water in the distance. A lake. It's beautiful."

"I still say it looks like a prison. A country-club prison."

She gave him a thin smile. "If you're going to hang out with me, Jake, you'd better fix the cranky attitude."

"Yeah. Whatever."

"You promised," she said again, knowing full well a promise meant a lot to Jake.

"All right, everyone," Sandra the guide instructed them from the front of the bus. "Let's file off now. Please enter the Welcome Center through the yellow door, and wait there in the large central reception hall. Your luggage will be delivered to your individual cabins, so you don't have to worry about that, but please have your name badges with you."

"Prison," Jake muttered as he held out a hand to help Zoë down the steps of the bus. But he waited for her to go first, through the requisite yellow door into a charming stone building that seemed to have been constructed of the same stuff as the fence surrounding the camp.

Before she had even cleared the doors, Zoë saw a few golf carts piled high with luggage speed off in one direction as Sandra and the bus blasted back out through the gates. The electric doors closed quickly behind the bus, giving the whole thing an air of finality. No changing her mind now. She was hitched to Jake for the duration.

She slipped her hand into his. Nowhere else she'd rather be.

But a little voice somewhere in the farthest regions of her brain whispered, *Zoë, don't you think you're moving kind of fast here? He's looking for some other woman. He's only tolerating you because you're his cover. How crazy are you, girl?*

"Not that crazy," she muttered under her breath.

"Did you say something?"

"Nope." She smiled up at him. It was an adventure. It was her destiny. Whatever happened now, she was ready. Even if her destiny was to have a fun week with a cute cop and then head home alone. Yep. She was ready.

Inside the stone building, they were shepherded into a large, woodsy room with a high-beamed ceiling. As Jake checked out the other couples, Zoë looked around at their surroundings, deciding it was a case of "so far, so good." No tents. No portable potties. Just a real, well-tended building with a nice attention to detail. Okay, so the security level seemed strange, since the room was rimmed and all the exits were blocked by EJ personnel, dressed identically in fashionable athletic wear, with drawstring pants and little hooded jackets with the now-familiar EJ logo on the breast. And they all had small microphones crooked over their ears and over their cheeks, with wires running down inside their hoodies.

Zoë narrowed her eyes. Maybe Jake was right. They did look like a bunch of guards. Guarding a spa?

But a man slightly older than the others, with a gleaming bald head and an earring, called them to attention. The name tag around his neck, just like theirs, read "Tommy." He didn't look like a Tommy. He looked like Mr. Clean. Or maybe Yul Brynner in that creepy movie about the amusement park where everyone turned out to be robots. Zoë shuddered. She didn't need to be thinking their group leader was an automaton.

"Welcome to the Explorer's Journey!" Tommy announced, sounding all hearty and happy, pressing his hands together in a prayerful gesture. "I am your group leader. You are going to become very well acquainted with me while you're here. Although not as well as you will become acquainted with each other, if you know what I mean."

He chuckled, and most of the people in the room ho-ho'ed right along. But Tommy's voice and manner were so slick and salesy that Zoë found him suspicious. She glanced over at Jake to see if he was going to make some crack about Mr. Clean, but his mouth was firmly closed.

"We are so pleased," Tommy added, "that you have all chosen to spend your honeymoons here with us, and we hope you will make the most of your journey. Our goal is for you to discover all the tools you will need to find true marital bliss, to commit yourselves to working together, always together, toward becoming the real partners that you can be. We want you to move forward, in love and in sync, as you follow your path together. Our motto here is Together Forever, No Matter What. In fact, you will see that motto painted on the wall in each building you will be in this week. It's that important to us. So I would like to see a show of hands, please. How many of you are willing to work with us toward achieving that goal? How many of you are willing to make that *forever* commitment?"

Every hand in the room shot up. Except hers. Even Jake had his hand in the air, although not very far. She felt like a real liar promising to work on Together Forever, No Matter What, when she was here under false pretenses. Forever? She didn't know if the two of them would last through tonight without killing each other or Jake trying to escape over the wall because she couldn't control herself and jumped his bones. But with a gulp, Zoë got with the program and flashed her hand up, too.

"Why don't you each repeat the mantra, please?" Tommy instructed.

Dutifully they all rumbled, "Together forever, no matter what."

Tommy nodded approvingly. "While you are here, we want you focused on each other and the tasks at hand. So we ask that you not use cell phones or radios or televisions or computers or organizers or anything like that. They will be confiscated if we see them. There are no in and out privileges. Now that you've all made the commitment, we expect you to stay here for the whole program."

"Confiscating cell phones and computers? No in and out privileges?" Jake whispered.

"Shh," she ordered.

Tommy's voice swelled. "As you begin this journey,

we want you to own the journey, embrace the journey, become one with the journey."

"That is the stupidest thing—"

Zoë pinched his arm.

"In order to accomplish that, we feel it's important to shed your baggage from the outside world," Tommy went on in the same gung-ho tone. "We want you to look at each other with new eyes, to leave behind any negative patterns from the past."

Well, that was one thing they had going for them—no negative patterns from the past. Because they had no past. *Score one for our side,* Zoë thought.

"In our busy lives, many of us worry about shallow things like designer labels and expensive shoes," Tommy continued, doing a tsk-tsk thing.

But at the mention of the word "shoes," Zoë remembered the one bit of info Jake had let drop, and she tuned out to do a quick survey of the footwear in the room. Nope. She checked each and every foot, and there was nary a sparkly plastic sandal. She waggled her eyebrows at Jake, trying to let him know she was on the case. But he just gave her a funny look that told her he had no idea what she was doing.

Shoes, she mouthed.

"What?"

"Shoes!"

"Excuse me." The words came from Tommy, but everyone in the room was staring at them. "It's important that you pay attention. We wouldn't want you to miss anything before we even get started."

Aw, jeez. Singled out as a behavior problem already. First the hand and now this.

Tommy raised his voice a notch. "Here at the Explorer's Journey, we're going to cut right to the heart of matters, without wasting time on appearances. So we're going to ask you to shed the clothes you came in and put them aside, just as you put aside all your old bad habits, *before* you fully enter your journey." His cheesy grin widened. "It's time to drop your masks. Cast off your baggage. And start anew."

Jake raised an eyebrow at her, and she knew what he was thinking. What was this all about? Shedding their clothes? As in, *nude*? Here? Now? In front of everyone?

Tommy picked up his pace. "We're going to give each of you some new clothing to wear while you're here. Nothing fancy, because that's not our way. Just comfortable and easy and simple."

Phew. She didn't even look at Jake this time.

"So please line up at the window where you see AJ waving his hand," Tommy went on, pointing to the far wall. "Snag your new garments, take your partner and find the changing room with your names on the door. Once you've changed, hurry right back. We're going to do a short serenity exercise and then an introductory test of your empathy. After that, you can separate, to go to your own villas and begin your honeymoons." He waggled his eyebrows in a meaningful and leering sort of way, so that every single person in the room knew what he meant. There were even a few giggles as people hot-footed it into line.

Get through this nonsense pronto, ol' Tommy boy was saying, *so you can get right on to the steamy honeymoon sex.*

Zoë tried not to think about it. She had other things to worry about at the moment. Like those tiny dressing rooms around the outside of the hall, where everyone else had toddled off, two by two, perfectly happy to strip in the presence of loved ones. She gave Jake a wary glance. Sure, it was a relief not to be thinking they had to do this program in the nude. And it sounded all fine and good to shed your baggage and start anew. But were the two of them really expected to go into a tiny room and strip?

"What if I like what I have on?" Zoë asked no one in particular, as surprised as Jake was that *she* was the one raising objections.

"Go on," another of the drones in sweats told them, making shooing motions with his hands. His smile was so wide it looked as if it had been cut out and pasted on. "The exercise suits are great. You'll love them."

"What's the problem? So we all have to wear the same thing. Big deal. Just like being on a team, going to camp, being in prison," Jake murmured into her ear. "But hey, I'm blending."

Everyone else was doing it. They were the only ones left. There was no choice.

Nobody told me I was going to have to strip in front of him! she thought darkly. Under her breath, she repeated, "You're with Jake. He's a stand-up guy. Nothing will happen. He'll close his eyes."

Except she'd already shown the stand-up guy half her butt and most of her breasts, fallen asleep on the stand-up guy, kissed the stand-up guy and felt up the stand-up guy's thigh. How much worse could it get?

She eyed Jake. A lot worse.

So there they were, last in line, as the grinning guy behind the counter sized them up and handed over matching pastel zip-front jackets with EJ logos on the chest, shirts and drawstring pants, just like all the Explorer's Journey personnel were wearing. They even got brand-new Nikes in their sizes and socks with an EJ logo on the ankle.

Zoë's tracksuit was lavender. Jake got blue. Some of

the other couples were already emerging from their dressing rooms, happy with the stylish, comfy outfits, giggling and admiring each other.

With a deep breath for courage, clutching the garments, Zoë entered the dressing room right behind Jake. Of course it said "Zoë and Wylie" on the door, but other than that, it was ordinary enough, a small plain room with nothing but a short wooden bench in the center and a basket at the end of the bench with a sign that said "Leave all street clothes and personal items here."

"I don't know," she said doubtfully, dangling a soft jersey tank top from one hand and a pair of what looked like yoga pants from the other. She didn't have any objection to the things themselves. It was just...how was she going to get into them? "I like the fabric. I guess that's good."

But how in the world was she going to get out of her peasant blouse and slip this top on without flashing anything at Jake? And why had she chosen today of all days not to wear a bra? Was it hot in here? Was she starting to sweat?

"Jake, do you really think we should do this?" she asked, stalling big time. So far, she had been the one who kept telling him this newlywed masquerade was no risk, no danger, no problem. But contemplating baring her all, one item of clothing at a time, in this tiny room, with Jake watching every move... She felt like screaming.

"I'm game," he said in this arrogant, devil-may-care voice that frayed her nerves even more. How dare he be unconcerned? He leaned casually into one wall. "Come on, Zoë. This is your program. Get with it. And I'm the good guy, remember? Nothing to fear from me." He smiled. "I'm willing to get naked for the good of the show if you are."

"You are not!" Her own words, thrown back at her, except she'd volunteered to kiss him, not "get naked" for him!

"You're not willing to embrace the journey? Become one with the journey?" he said mockingly.

He was probably just testing her again, trying to scare her off. What was she supposed to do? "You're going to have to..." She chewed her lip, making a circular motion with one finger. "Turn around. And no peeking."

She spun around herself, staring straight into a knotty-pine wall. Gingerly she pulled off her blouse and pants, quickly crossing her arms over her breasts. Where had she dropped that tank top? She picked up the top and tried to figure out the front from the back. No tag. Oh, hell. The sides looked exactly the same. She slammed it on over her head. Good enough.

Behind her, she could hear him shifting around, too. Maybe by the time she looked back, he would be totally dressed and she wouldn't have to blush or drool or anything embarrassing.

She sent a tiny glance over her shoulder. He had discarded his jacket and T-shirt, but he was putting the shirt back on again. Two inches of tanned male midriff, and her cheeks were already flaming. And why was he putting his shirt back on? She cleared her throat, edging around. "Wh-what are you doing?"

"Okay, I give. I'm not willing to get naked. I lied." His face was grimmer than it had been at any time so far. "This is ridiculous. All of it. So I say we wait till they all dress and come out and then we sneak away from here."

"But there's no leaving," Zoë reminded him. "The bus left. It only comes back to pick us up at the end of the program, and there's no other transport in or out. It's part of the plan, remember? We're supposed to be committed."

"Anyone who goes through with this junk should be committed."

Zoë felt like smacking him. She was standing there wearing nothing but a tank top and her underpants, for goodness' sake. Now was not the time for this! "You promised to blend. And you said you were game and to get with the program."

"I changed my mind. I want out."

"Come on, Jake. Think of your mission to find Cinderella with the sparkly ho' shoes," she snapped. "I'm sure you can get your clothes off fast enough if you think of her."

"It's not because I'm afraid to strip, damn it. I've changed my clothes in more locker rooms than you'll ever see in your life. It's because I don't want to stand here and…"

His brows lowered. His jaw clenched. His eyes were firmly fixed on the place where her top gaped above the line of her bikini underwear, revealing a whole lot of skin, from belly button to hip and thigh. She could feel herself flush with hot color. Damn pale skin. She was probably as red as her hair. Blushing was way too easy. And too obvious. She snatched up her pants from the bench, sort of awkwardly holding them in front of her.

He gritted out, "Forget it." His eyes burned into her as he reached for the hem of his shirt. He yanked it over his head.

"Oh." Zoë felt the need to sit down. *Now.*

She practically collapsed onto the bench. Ridged muscle. Sculpted chest, firmly chiseled arms, flat stomach with just a tracing of fine brown hair that led a path into his jeans. Hard man, up and down. Big, hard man who made her knees weak and her mouth water. She bit down onto her already bruised lip, hoping the pain would distract her. But her gaze was stuck there on his bare torso, as trapped as the air in her lungs that couldn't seem to move.

His hand slid to the top button on his jeans. Pop.

"I'll just..." She choked. "I'll just turn around."

She spun around on that bench so fast she got a splinter in her bottom through her underpants. Somehow she managed to scramble into the yoga pants, to find the jacket and to jam her arms into the sleeves. Three seconds, tops. She put on her socks and shoes, testing the feel of the sneakers. Good enough. But she could still hear the sound of his unzipping and rustling and stripping back there.

Torture, plain and simple.

Fully clothed, she stood up from the bench, dumping her old garments into the basket. "So, you ready?" she inquired, trying to make her voice sound more casual and less rattled, while the image of Jake's bare chest and his hand, snaking over to the button on his jeans, remained branded in her brain.

Mostly looking at the floor, she sent her gaze skittering over to his side of the room. He was turned away, but she saw his back, covered in a sea-blue-knit T-shirt that draped his broad shoulders nicely. But he lost his grip on the drawstring pants just when she thought it was safe to turn. She saw about half a second of his whole beautiful bottom, rounded, firm, perfectly formed, before he caught the fabric and tugged it back into place.

It was like looking right into the sun. Jake had a great butt. One of the all-time-great butts. She gulped. She was going to be haunted for the rest of her life.

Jake didn't wear underwear. No tighty whities. No boxers. Nothing at all. Why not? Who cared why not? He didn't. She knew that for sure. *Jake didn't wear underwear.*

Staring at the floor, Zoë gulped for air, feeling for the wall for support. His bare pecs and abs, his butt, all within the last five minutes. And it was her own stupid fault, for yelling at him and forcing him to go along.

The good news was, she got to spend a whole lot of time up close and personal with the most fabulous man she'd ever seen. The bad news was, she wasn't allowed to touch him, no matter how up close and personal it got.

How was she ever going to survive this journey?

6

JAKE WAS ALREADY LOSING his mind and they were barely started on their road to exploration. He'd had plenty of exploration so far, thanks.

He blamed Zoë. *Nah.* He shook his head. That was the problem. He didn't blame Zoë. He liked Zoë. A little too much, especially considering how nutty she was. Although she'd been acting strange, even for her, since they got out of that dressing room. Before she'd been all perky and chatty; now she was subdued, a little shy, not exactly meeting his gaze. What was that all about? And why did figuring it out seem a lot more interesting than searching for the missing con woman who was pretending to be his half sister?

Now that they'd all handed over their street clothes and were shod in the standard-issue footwear, it was even more frustrating, because he couldn't check for too-tight jeans or sparkly sandals, and none of the women in the room looked that much like the one in the fuzzy photos. He could've used a handy roster or some list, so he could start matching names to suspects, but none of the personnel seemed to have anything like that, and pestering them only made them suspicious. They'd also made him leave all of his things, including his notebook and pen, in the basket with his clothes. Which didn't make him happy in the least.

While they fed them some sort of vegetarian lunch

buffet full of sprouts and cucumbers and carrot juice, he'd tried to scope out the name tags, but they'd brought the lights down, making it awfully dim in there.

Not that it mattered. So far, this had wild-goose chase written all over it. Why would any self-respecting con woman sign up for a marriage encounter group, anyway?

"I'm going to kill my old man," he muttered. As soon as they broke up this little opening-night shindig, he was going to look for a way out. Because he wasn't at all sure he could keep going, keep pretending, when Zoë kept making him crazy.

Like that whole dressing-room thing. No matter how many times he'd told himself it was no big deal, it had turned into a very big, very disturbing deal. He was a sedate guy. Even keel. In control. But not around Zoë. Jake took a deep breath. Not around Zoë.

Which only meant he shouldn't be around her. If it took going over the wall to make that happen, then he'd do it, whether it meant letting his father down or not.

But first he had to get through couples meditation, whatever that was.

"Everyone, please sit cross-legged on the pillows on the floor, facing your partner," Tommy, the ridiculous Captain Picard look-alike, told them. "Please scoot as close as you can get, knee to knee, and place your hands flat against each other's. Not clasped, but flat. Yes, like that."

Jake shuffled around, trying not to look at Zoë, which was kind of hard considering she was about an inch away, straight in front of him. As instructed, he slid his palms up against hers. Her hands felt warm and soft and small, and her eyes had this funny sparkle in them. She'd put her hair back into the braids, but there were little red-gold wisps escaping at her temples and the nape of her neck, and he had to fight to stop himself from pulling a hand free and stroking the stray tendrils back into place. She chewed her lip, and he could see the little tooth mark in the soft part of her bottom lip. His gut clenched. That's where he'd bit her. *Oh, hell.*

"Good, good," Tommy said encouragingly. "Close your eyes, please."

Jake was only too happy to oblige on that one.

"Breathe in," Tommy said in a hypnotic sort of voice. "Breathe out. Deeply. Very deeply."

He wanted them to take ten seconds to inhale and another ten to exhale, which seemed excessive to Jake, but what did he know? He just breathed. Hey, it was supposed to be calming. All to the good. Even if he could feel Zoë breathing, too, right through his hands. It was the strangest, most intimate thing. With his eyes closed, his knees and his hands up against hers, it was as if he could feel Zoë vibrating through his whole body.

"Now please take your right hand, reach across and place your palm against your partner's abdomen, below the rib cage," Tommy instructed.

Just when he thought it couldn't get any worse. Gingerly Jake slid his hand across to Zoë's waist, and she did the same to him.

"Feel the air move in and out. You should feel your partner's diaphragm expand under your hand as you inhale together. Can you feel it?"

Oh, yeah, he could feel it. Although he wasn't sure his diaphragm had anything to do with what he was feeling. This went a little lower.

He tried to keep his fingers on the soft cotton of her tank top, but as she breathed, the fabric rose, and he could feel her hot, smooth, bare skin under his hand.

Somehow he managed to take in air, forcing himself to think about baseball and fishing and rock climbing. Anything but his hand and her hand and the way his body was responding. Thank God, the room was dim. At this rate, he was going to have to borrow the pillow he was sitting on and plaster it over the front of his pants just to get out of here.

"Are you all feeling relaxed and serene?" the idiot in charge asked gently.

Relaxed? He was holding himself so rigid he was afraid he was going to turn to stone. Or maybe he already had.

"Good, good," Tommy murmured. "We recommend you perform this serenity exercise together every night. And it's particularly effective done in the nude. We prefer you do it clothed in group sessions, but nude is fine, if that's better for you."

Jake's eyes flew open. He choked and snatched his hand away from her stomach, staring into Zoë's rosy, overheated face and wide green eyes. She pulled both her hands up to her chin and clasped them there.

She knew exactly what he was thinking. Fully clothed, sitting up, with a swarm of other people in the room, they should've been safe. But their minds were both filled with images of slick, hot, naked skin and entwined body parts. They'd kissed exactly once, and they were already itching to turn to about page 150 of the Kama Sutra. One more second of her hand right there, so close to the drawstring on his pants, so close, and he truly would've knocked her back onto the floor and made love to her for about an hour, no matter who was watching.

Zoë gasped, tipping backward off her pillow, which was exactly what he had been imagining doing to her.

"I—I'm sorry," he mumbled, reaching for her hand. "I didn't mean—"

"No, no, you didn't do anything," she interrupted.

"Are you two having trouble with the exercise?" Tommy asked, bending his bald head in toward them.

"It's me." Zoë jumped to her feet. "I'm not feeling well, and..."

That was Jake's cue to stand, too, to come around behind her and pretend to be solicitous. "Are you all right, sweetheart?" All he was really doing was hiding the raging evidence of his unfettered desire, and they both knew it. Thank God, it was dark in here.

"I'm fine, really," Zoë stammered. "I think I'm hungry and tired, and I felt a little faint with all that breathing."

"That's all right," Tommy said kindly. "We have one more exercise, more of a game, really, and then we'll be breaking, so you can all, uh, take a nap or have some dinner or whatever suits you." Under his breath, he told Zoë, "It won't be long till you two can be alone."

The creep actually winked at Zoë, and Jake felt like punching him. What he and Zoë did or didn't do when they were alone—and Jake had no intention of doing anything—it was none of Tommy boy's business. He stayed where he was behind Zoë, but he put a protective arm around her, as if to signal Tommy to back off.

She turned into him and whispered, "Jake, maybe you should take off your jacket and, you know, tie it around your waist. You look a little...hot. Like you need to take off your jacket."

Okay, so they both knew what was going on here. Jake didn't say a word, just unzipped his hooded jacket and looped it around his waist, hiding the evidence. He felt like a twelve-year-old. And it only made it worse that Zoë knew, too.

"Everyone," their group leader called out, moving away, "if I could have your attention, please? Husbands, if you could all move to this side of the room, and wives, if you could scoot over to the opposite side. Thank you."

As the lights came up, Jake ambled over to the wall and took a seat, pulling his knees up as he sat on the floor. *Okay, okay, get a grip. You're not touching her. You're not even near her.* But he kept Zoë in sight.

He had enough of his brain still functioning to realize he should be more concerned about reading name tags and putting names to faces, to make some steps toward finding his quarry. But his head was still full of Zoë and the intimacy of that damn breathing exercise. He couldn't think clearly.

"Good, good," Tommy said again. "Beth is passing out a short form for you to fill out. This is an empathy test. We have six simple questions for you, to see how much you know about your partner. After we see how you all do, we will know more about what we'll need to work on this week. So, if you could each take a test and a pen, you can get started."

Jake didn't like the sound of this. When he got a gander at the questions, he liked it even less. But at least it was mundane enough to give him a breather, to get his body back under control.

Sure, he could handle penciling in his occupation and his favorite food, and even his personal hero and greatest fear, given a few minutes to think about it. But then he had to answer the same six questions again. About Zoë.

This was some freaky, boring, navel-gazing version of *The Newlywed Game*. Instead of "Where will your wife say you most like to make whoopee?" it was "What will your wife say is the one thing in life you value most?" He hated when people asked him stuff like this, anyway, and then, when you factored in that he was supposed to be a mind reader and figure out what Zoë would answer...

He glanced over at her. She was frowning down at her paper, too. Oh, man. They were going to get every single question wrong. And then what?

When he contemplated the half of the page that related to his own tastes and views, Jake considered trying to second-guess what Zoë might think he would answer, but that got way too complicated. Besides, he hadn't a clue how her mind worked.

"I could know her for a hundred years and still not get her," he said under his breath. Zoë was just plain wacked. Who could figure her out?

So he answered as honestly as he could, not spending a whole lot of time on it. And then he stared at her, just all-out stared, as if that might help him somehow discover whether she was a first or second-born and whether she might like ice cream better than broccoli. Not a chance.

Finally he scrawled an answer in each blank, coming up with any old thing. First, he had a pretty good hunch she made her living reading tarot cards. The cards, the candles... She had denied it, but she'd said she worked at home, and what else could she do in that funky apartment?

So he wrote in "professional psychic" for her occupation. That sounded better than fortune-teller. Off the top of his head, he decided she was so goofy she had to be a youngest child and that someone like her would value something sappy like sharing. Nah. World peace. Biggest fear? How about nuclear war? Meanness? Yeah, people being mean to each other. That sounded like something that would tick her off. Although she *had* worked up a certain indignation over the idea of sparkly plastic shoes, as he recalled. He smiled. You just never knew what would get under a woman's skin. Especially one as off-the-wall as Zoë.

Her favorite food...well, he was just going to have to pick one. He sent her another glance. That red hair and the light dusting of freckles across her nose made him think of strawberries. So he took the plunge and added "strawberries" to his list. And her hero was... Mother Teresa. Yeah, that sounded about right. Feeling pretty proud of himself for coming up with plausible answers, he waited to hear the results.

"All right then." Tommy was positively beaming. "Please fold your paper so that your answers are not visible, and then return to sit by your spouse. We'll go around the room and see how everyone did." As people shuffled back into place, Tommy leaned down close enough to read the name tags on the couple closest to him. "Ron and Tori. Why don't you tell us what you said?"

Tori? Jake's ears perked up. Neither Ron nor Tori looked remarkable, but the name was close enough. And the body shape and foot size looked possible, too. Mentally he recorded Tori as a definite maybe. Both Tori and Ron were toned and fit, bouncy, like a couple of gymnasts or something. And they had a smug air about them. When they read aloud their answers, Jake understood why they looked smug. They got every question right on the empathy exam, reeling off their answers with the efficiency of a well-oiled machine. Tori and Ron basked in approval from Tommy, the leader, and all the other personnel, who clapped enthusiastically for their perfect score.

Losers. Who cared if you scored right on an empathy exam?

As couple after couple revealed their answers, he noted that almost everyone did very well. Not a lot of slackers here. The spotlight wound around to his part of the room, closer and closer, and Jake felt apprehensive and conspicuous. Would he look like a jerk and have every answer wrong? Would Zoë?

"Zoë and...Jake?" Tommy prompted, standing right over them. "Your turn."

Jake set his jaw. "You first," he mumbled, signaling to Zoë.

She frowned. "No, you."

There was a long pause. "Jake?" Tommy inquired. "What did you pick for Zoë?"

Might as well get it over with. No one had ever said he was a coward. "I said Zoë is a professional psychic," he announced, as she made a small choking noise. "She is a youngest child, she values world peace, she fears people who are mean, she likes strawberries, and her hero is Mother Teresa."

And he just realized he had made her sound like a Miss America candidate. Or a Playboy centerfold.

"Zoë? What did you say?" Tommy asked.

"Well, he was right about the strawberries," she said hopefully, pointing to the word on her paper.

He supposed he should be happy he got that one. But all he could think about was how much of an idiot he was going to look like for missing all the rest. Especially since the lone right answer was pure coincidence.

Tommy asked, "And the rest?"

She shook her head. "The occupation question is complicated for me, so that's not his fault," she said quickly, and he knew she was trying to cover and make it sound not so bad for the rest of the people in the room. She wasn't trying to be nice to him, not with the cranky look she sent him when she thought no one was looking. "I mean, I know why he put that down, but I actually do more than one thing, and I just happened to choose one of the other jobs. Which would be, um, dance teacher. That's what I wrote. I mean, I don't actually make a living at it, but I do teach modern dance to seniors. I like that one the best of my sort of patchwork of jobs, so I wrote that down."

"That's fine, Zoë. We don't need the whole explanation. There are no right or wrong answers here."

Oh, yeah, sure. Only everyone else in the room got everything right, while Jake didn't even know his "wife's" occupation. And smug know-it-alls like Ron and Tori now knew he didn't know.

Meanwhile, what did she say she did? She taught seniors how to dance? Jake was suddenly very sorry he'd never asked her more about herself. How could he not have asked what she did?

"I'm an only child, so technically, he's right. I mean, only, youngest, oldest, what's the diff?" she went on, speeding up, not really looking at him. "I put down, well, true love as what I value, and my greatest fear is..." Her voice dropped even lower. "Um, I said it was watching the love of my life walk away from me."

Aw, jeez. Which was exactly what her ex-fiancé had done, right? Jake was starting to feel like such a heel here. He had mistreated and yelled at—and lusted after—a woman who was so vulnerable and sweet that her greatest fear was being walked out on. He couldn't have felt lower if he'd tried.

Ah, but he could.

"And what about your hero, Zoë?" Tommy asked.

This time she looked right at Jake. She even had a little smile playing around her lips. "My husband, of course," she said sweetly. If there was any edge of sarcasm there, he was the only one who caught it.

My husband is my hero. If he could've slid right through the floorboards into a pit somewhere under the middle of Wisconsin, Jake would've gladly taken that slide right now.

She chose me? he thought. *She doesn't even know me.*

Or maybe she meant the other guy, Wylie, the one who was supposed to be her husband? Nope. She'd said Wylie was a lowlife. She definitely meant him. But he was perplexed and bewildered. Why would she choose *him?* It had to be hypothetical, like she thought if she had a husband, he would be her hero. That had to be the explanation.

"All right, Zoë," Tommy announced. "Now why don't you tell us what you wrote down in your other column, for Jake?"

She hesitated. Jake waited. "Jake is a policeman," she began, still looking right at him. She lifted her chin. "A supervisor of tactical teams."

How did she remember that? Okay, she knew he was a cop. But his exact title? He'd only said it once. She was just showing off.

"You're the oldest child," she went on, gaining volume and momentum, speaking with a certain amount of defiance. "I didn't know exactly how to put what you value, but it's like being loyal and good and true, and always doing the right thing. I think your greatest fear would be disappointing someone, and your hero is your father. Oh, and your favorite food is steak."

Jake just sat there, blinking. How the hell did she do that? Was she really psychic?

"Well?" Tommy asked.

"She's right. On all counts." Frowning, he held up his paper so that anyone who wanted to could see Zoë had scored a bull's-eye on every one.

"Good job, Zoë," Tommy and his troops chorused, and everyone gave her polite applause. "Maybe after this week, Jake will know you as well as you know him."

Jake narrowed his eyes at his paper. How did she do that? He couldn't wait to get her out of there and make her tell him the trick.

Even more than that, he felt angry and ashamed. He didn't appreciate flunking anything. But he felt a lot worse right now, knowing that he hadn't known a thing about Zoë while she'd had him down cold.

"Thank you, everyone," Tommy called out. "That concludes the planned part of tonight's program. As you exit, please see the facilitators by the door for your room assignments. We invite you to stroll down to your cabins, settle in, enjoy yourselves. We will see you all again first thing in the morning, when our real work will begin."

Still feeling humiliated, Jake lurked safely behind Zoë as she collected the key and map to their cabin.

Couples were tripping down the paths that led out from the Welcome Center in every direction.

Jake glowered at the procession of happy couples racing to get behind closed doors and leap into marital bliss. Laughing, smiling, positively romping, they were all acting like a bunch of saps.

Zoë started to go left, stepped back into him, went right, and then stopped. "We're in one of the hillside villas," she said, handing him the map. "Number eleven. But I can't quite figure out how to get there from here."

"Oh, so Miss Smarty Pants can read minds, just not a map, is that it?"

Zoë stopped. "Are you mad at me for getting all the answers right, Jake?" she asked in a superior tone. "Are we feeling a tad defensive?"

"No," he snapped.

She just looked at him.

"Okay, yes. Yes, I am," he admitted. "I should've known better than to pretend to be married to someone when I don't even know what she does for a living. Do you really do that? The dance thing with the seniors, I mean? Or was that as much of a lie as me being your hero? And how did you know all that stuff about me?"

"I should be the one who's mad. You realize that, right? If I really was married to you, I would be devastated that my husband was that selfish and so much of a..." She broke off, she took a little huffy breath, and her cheeks got pinker. "That my husband was a nonempathetic slug."

"So far, if people like Ron and Tori are any example, empathy ain't anything I want."

"Baloney!" She grabbed the map back and started down the nearest path.

"That's the wrong way."

"It is not."

"Oh, yes, it is." He stayed where he was, pointing to a carved wooden sign nailed to a post right where the paths diverged. There were two choices and two arrows, and the one for villas went the other direction. "Lake cabins that way, hillside villas this way."

"Oh, all right!" She backtracked and headed down the

right path, shoving the map at him. "Lead on, Mac-Slug."

"What's that supposed to mean?"

"Shakespeare, you know."

"I'm on a bogus honeymoon with a bunch of people who think it's fun to spend the first night of their honeymoons taking a damn test, and if that's not bad enough, I'm stuck with a woman who's quoting Shakespeare at me. This just keeps getting better and better," he said acidly.

"Oh, yeah? Well, *I'm* on a bogus honeymoon with a man who doesn't know a thing about me and doesn't seem to care enough to fake it properly. And this person I'm stuck with? He doesn't even know that the word MacSlug isn't from Shakespeare," she shot back, stomping down the path ahead of him. "The quote is 'Lead on, Macduff,' okay? MacSlug was all mine." Under her breath, but loud enough that he could hear it, she muttered, "I don't think I can be on a honeymoon with a man who doesn't know that MacSlug isn't Shakespeare."

Jake tried not to laugh. Suddenly his mood had improved a hundred percent. And all because calm, centered Zoë was losing her temper. Why did that amuse him so much? Maybe because she kept harping at him about not being serene enough. Had her serenity taken a hit, too, during couples meditation and the empathy exam?

"Don't get too far ahead," he warned, ambling behind her. "Zoë, take a left when we get to a fork, okay? We go around the back side of the lake and up the hill."

He glanced down at the map. So far, they were at least headed in the general direction of Villa Number eleven. The last thing they needed to do was get lost. He was pretty sure there were bears and coyotes and timber wolves running around in Wisconsin. He doubted any were crazy enough to wander into the Explorer's Journey, but you never knew.

She took the left turn as ordered, still well ahead of him, but then she halted in the middle of the path. "What was that?" she whispered.

"What?"

"I heard something breathing," she confided, her eyes wide. "Like, panting. And sort of...giggling. Are there bears here?"

"Bears don't giggle." Jake ducked around her, taking a few steps off the main path, onto a tiny, narrow trail that curved around into the underbrush.

But then he caught sight of something flesh-tone bouncing up and down between the branches. He stopped where he stood. It didn't take a detective to figure this one out, what with the giggling, and all manner of sex-crazed newlyweds running around this place.

He turned quickly, catching Zoë before she got any closer. "It's not a bear."

But the panting and moaning got a whole lot louder all of a sudden. Leaves were shaking, a woman's voice was shrieking, and the words "Yes! Yesss! Yessss!" blasted from the not-so-hidden hideaway back in the woods.

Not exactly sure what to do, Jake gazed down at Zoë, still blocking her way. Awkwardly he offered, "I guess somebody couldn't wait till they got back to their cabin."

Zoë's eyes went wide as the shrieks of pleasure got even louder and more sustained. "Holy moly. She's having fun."

"We should probably...move on. Back on the path."

"Yeah. Probably."

Neither stirred for a second, until Jake spun her around and guided her away from the excitement as quietly as possible. Why he didn't want to embarrass people who were tacky enough to be doing the nasty in such a stupid place, he had no idea. But there it was. Jake Calhoun, Boy Scout.

Safely on the way toward their cabin, Zoë broke the silence. "Well, that was interesting. They were sure exposing some major skin there. I hope they don't get poison ivy. Poison oak. Bug bites. Could be dangerous."

"Chiggers," he supplied helpfully.

He could see her lips quivering, and he knew she was trying hard not to snicker. "You are so hoping they *do* get chiggers, aren't you?" she asked.

"No comment."

She covered her mouth with one hand, but her laughter spilled out, anyway. And then she slowed up. "Will you look at that?"

What did she see? He followed the direction her finger was pointing. There was a small sign discreetly posted near the edge of the path, where a smaller trail disappeared into the woods. "Lovers' Bower. Privacy Please. What the hell does that mean?"

Zoë reached for the map, scrutinizing it. "There are lovers' bowers and lovers' overlooks all over the place. Even a lovers' *swing*. See? Over here, not far from the lake cabins."

A lovers' swing? He could only imagine. But she was right. There were tiny hearts scattered all over the map, marking "private spots where you and your partner can commune with nature." "This place is nuts," he muttered.

"Maybe just romantic," Zoë said with a smile.

"Uh-huh." As they trudged up the path, every step bringing them that much closer to Villa Number eleven, Jake tried to block his ears from any more maddening sounds of lovemaking back in the nooks and crannies of the woods. But every rustle, every sigh of wind put him on red alert.

Picking up the pace, he realized he was actually starting to look forward to getting to their own little cabin. Not for the same reason as anyone else here on the Explorer's Journey, of course. Not to shut the door, turn down the lights and get to the lovemaking.

Nope. He needed refuge. Badly. Somewhere where he wouldn't have to hear heavy breathing and think about sex every single minute.

He slid a glance over at Zoë, who would be walking into that refuge along with him. Oh, yeah. Zoë. Was there even a chance in hell of any place they shared being peaceful?

Zoë. The woman whose very breathing was erotic.

Nope. Not a chance in hell.

7

ZOË WAS THRILLED with her first glimpse of their hill-side villa. From the front, it looked like a quaint little cottage, with a simple deck and some Adirondack furniture out front. But you could tell there was more to it on the back side, tapering down the hill.

"Looks great," she murmured, patting her jacket pockets for the key.

It had been a long walk from the Welcome Center, and she was ready to sit down somewhere quiet and private, where she wouldn't have to worry about erotic oohs or aahs or a full view of people's bouncing body parts peeping out at every corner. Yikes. She wasn't one to judge other people's choices, and if they wanted to go at it like greased weasels under bushes and trees, it was none of her business. But in the state she was in, she also didn't need to see it happening right in front of her eyes.

She took the steps up onto the front deck, but she still hadn't found the key. She only had two pockets, so there wasn't much to search. Feeling quite put out with herself, she admitted, "Jake, I think I lost the key. I gotta tell you—I'm in no mood to walk back that whole way to get a new one."

"Don't worry." Jake reached around her to rattle the brass knob on the solid door. "I've busted a few burglars in my time. I know how it works."

But after searching his pockets for a handy lock pick

and, of course, finding nothing since all their personal belongings had been taken away when they changed clothes, Jake pushed and pulled at the knob for a few seconds. Not getting any give, he got a grim look on his face and backed up a few steps.

"Don't you dare," she warned, remembering his dramatic entrance to her apartment. And that door had been open. Was he planning to kick this one in? Zoë shook her head. "Whatever you're thinking, don't."

"How do you know what I'm thinking?" But he hopped off the deck and headed into the underbrush.

"Jake?" she called out. "Where are you going?"

No answer. Frustrated, she pounded the door with one fist, cursing herself for losing the key.

She could hear scuffling as he worked his way around to the back of the cabin. And about three minutes later, the door opened from the inside, and there was Jake, lounging in the doorway.

"How did you do that?" she asked.

"Back door. Downstairs. There's a walkout porch. Two levels."

And the back door was conveniently open? She didn't ask, just ducked inside.

"Two-level porch, huh?" Sounded cool to her, but Jake didn't seem impressed one way or the other. Maybe multilevel hillside villas were common for him. Well, not for her. Zoë tried not to let her jaw drop as Jake led the way back through a small but charming living room with a soaring ceiling and a stained-glass skylight. In it was a brick fireplace, already turned on so that tiny gas flames crackled invitingly behind glass doors, and an overstuffed leather chair and an ottoman set to face the fire. Though it was a tad muggy and warm outside, in here, even with a fire going, it was perfectly cool.

Ah. Air-conditioning. Zoë smiled. Communing with nature was great, but there was a lot to be said for good old air-conditioning.

As she ran her hand over the mantel, she realized that all the furnishings looked as if they were made of split logs, even the coffee table. There were also log shelves flanking the fireplace, where all sorts of nifty things were built in. CD player, TV, bookshelves... It was very nicely done, and she thought she could be very comfy here, with or without a newlywed husband. She spared a glance at Jake, who still had that gloomy expression on his face, and Zoë tried not to be irritated with him. She'd tried to let it go, but she was still mad.

Damn him, anyway. He'd gotten all the answers wrong on the empathy test. She had scored one hundred percent, and he had flunked. Big time. How nonempathetic could a guy be? How much clearer could he make it that he was not and never had been a good candidate for her true love?

So maybe the place would be better without the husband, if this was the best one she could muster.

Along the back of the room, there were lots of windows and a sliding glass door, and a beautiful view, too, with a wide vista of trees and the lake in the distance. She gazed at Jake. So moody. So unreadable. How could he not love this? How could he not be thanking his lucky stars he'd angled his way into paradise?

"Wow, this is great," Zoë said out loud, sparing a moment to take in the view. Rustic but still cushy. Classy. Lush. Yep. She liked it a lot.

She poked around the small kitchenette, noted the fruit-and-cheese basket sitting on the wet bar, with a note attached that read, "Welcome, Zoë and Wylie. We hope you will be very happy on your Explorer's Journey."

Great. Might as well send town criers to announce that she was a big fraud and a loser and had no business being on a honeymoon. Savagely she removed the note and threw it in the wastebasket, pulled a few grapes out of the basket and scarfed them as she went on with her search. The fridge was fully stocked with wine and bottled water and juice, and there were chocolate bars and other handy items laid out on the counter. She could really get accustomed to service like this.

"Very, very nice." Nibbling a grape, she came out from behind the counter, where she saw Jake leaning against a gnarled tree trunk, branches and all, that formed the newel post for the staircase leading to the upper level. She cast her eyes up the curving steps to the loft, wondering what was up there. The bedroom, no doubt. She hesitated. Sleeping arrangements were a tricky subject at the moment. Best not to bring that up.

Trying to think of something to say that did not include the word *bedroom*, she noted, "It's a lot nicer than my apartment."

"Wait till you see the back deck." Still leaning against the tree, Jake folded his arms over his chest, looking as if he were waiting for a reaction from her. Why? Something about the deck?

She marched across the room and slid open the door to see for herself. The deck curved downward, with two levels. And on this one, staring her right in the face, was a big ol' hot tub, carved right into the surface of the deck. A big, heart-shaped hot tub, built for two.

As heat and humidity once more hit her in the face, her mind filled with images of Jake, slipping sensuously into that hot tub, his skin wet and gleaming, with swirling water and rising bubbles parting around him, revealing more than they covered. Was she seeing the future? Or was this just wishful thinking? Either way, she was in deep water.

She gulped, taking a step back, away from the damn deck and its dangerous hot tub, almost crashing into Jake, who was much too close behind. He caught her neatly. He had a habit of doing that. But she stumbled away from his grasp.

"Uh, excellent," she managed, moving right past the hot tub and around the outside curve of the deck. "Gotta love a soak in a hot tub. Just the thing after a walk in the woods."

Not far away, there was a double hammock hanging from the exposed beams on the overhang. It had a note attached, too, and she could see from here that it said "Zoë and Wylie" on it. More communications for her and her ex-but-not-forgotten fiancé.

If she had gotten married after all, would she and Wylie have been here now, giggling and leaping into the hot tub or the hammock together? And why did that idea seem so ridiculous? Why did anything to do with Wylie—and especially making love—seem juvenile and stupid?

Even worse—why did the very thought of being here with Wylie seem like cheating on Jake? She hadn't even met Jake when she'd been with Wylie. She was *engaged* to Wylie. Nothing like that with Jake. Not even close.

It didn't matter. It still seemed like cheating every time she saw Wylie's name on a silly piece of paper. *You are nuts, girl*, she told herself. *Plain, freakin' nuts.*

"Warm out here," Zoë whispered, wiping moisture off her brow with the back of her hand, purposely not looking at Jake. She moved closer to the hammock, pulling off the note. Aloud, she read, "'Enjoy this hand-made, all-natural hammock, available for sale in the EJ gift shop. It's perfect for watching the luscious sunsets together. Jump in!' Well, isn't that nice? We can buy a hammock of our very own. If either of us needed a hammock. Or, you know, both of us."

She hadn't meant to say "both," which implied sharing the hammock. Really. There seemed to be peril around every turn in this place. But even after she'd finished her awkward little speech, Jake didn't say a word.

With the note still crumpled in her hand, Zoë cut around him, back into the house. Okay, as long as she got rid of all the references to Wylie, and Jake wasn't glowering at her, she definitely loved this place. But it was still a little *intimate*, what with all the stuff set up for two.

"What's downstairs?" she asked, almost afraid to look down the narrow, circular stairs. "Is that the way you came in?"

"Yeah. But there's not much down there. A fancy bathroom. Shelves full of towels. Jacuzzi, double shower, that kind of thing." His lips curved into a half smile. "And another shower outside on the lower deck. Like in a barrel or something. Very rustic."

More things built for happy couples who couldn't bear to be apart, even when they showered. "Well, staying here, we should definitely be...clean," she offered.

"Very."

She stood in the middle of the living room, biting her lip, gazing down at the fluffy white rug in front of the fireplace. It looked like every bad movie ever made where people rolled around naked on the floors of ski lodges. Okay, so she had to get her mind off all the erotic possibilities here. Plus, standing this close to the fire, it really was a little warm. Was there an on-off switch for this thing? "Where's the...?"

"Bed?" he supplied, which didn't help in the least. She'd been thinking about the switch for the fireplace. But he went on, "I'm guessing it's up there, in the loft." He paused. "You should really stop doing that."

She glanced up in surprise. "Stop doing what?"

"Chewing on your lip." He moved closer. "It's already..." He lifted a finger, tracing a rough spot in the center of her bottom lip. "Hurt."

"I have very resilient lips," she murmured, backing away.

Quickly, before he touched her again and she was tempted to knock him down onto the faux-fur rug and rip off every stitch of his baby-blue tracksuit, she ran up the stairs to the loft. It wasn't her smartest move, but it was the only available exit at that moment. And at least it was farther away from his hands.

Jake ambled up behind her, taking the steps more slowly.

When she got to the top and saw the bed, so big it took up most of the loft space all by itself, she had to laugh. Hard.

"It—it's *round*," she said between giggles. The bed was round? "And huge."

Trying not to cackle too loudly, she edged closer, giving it as wide a berth as she could manage in the small space. On the wall above the window, the Explorer's Journey motto had been painted in a swirling script. Together Forever, No Matter What, it said, with a few green leaves and vines painted around it. There was a closet and a chest of drawers opposite, even a small bathroom tucked behind the bedroom, but the bed dwarfed everything else. It wasn't so much the shape or the size as the color. And the drama. The thing was bright green, dripping with green silk leaves that cascaded from the ceiling, forming a sort of curtain around it. A canopy of leaves encasing the round bed.

"The rest of the place is classy, well, maybe except for the heart-shaped hot tub. But this..." Delicately she flicked a finger against a trailing vine. "Tarzan's bed?"

Jake stayed where he was on the top step. "That's obscene."

"Oh, come on. It's just for fun." She sat on the edge of the mattress, bouncing up and down. "Comfy, too."

Jake retreated two steps down the staircase. She half expected him to raise his fingers in the sign of a cross, as if he thought the bed was going to reach out and bite him.

"What, are you afraid the big, bad, round Tarzan bed is going to suck you in? Or I'm going to jump you and throw you on it? I already promised to keep my hands to myself," she reminded him. "I'm not the one who kissed you, am I? I'm not the one who got all stoked up during the serenity exercise."

"I don't want to discuss it." His expression and his voice were deadpan when he added, "But I would like to point out that you're the one who fell asleep in my lap. And you had your hand all over my thigh."

"I was just teasing you," she retorted.

"Uh-huh. Well, anyway, I'm not worried about anything happening in that hideous bed because I would never let it, anyway." He raked it and its leafy bower with a contemptuous glance. "It's just part and parcel of this whole place. And if you ask me, it's all..."

"What? Luxurious? Wonderful?" She was still kind of ticked off at him. She'd been nice enough to open up her honeymoon in this beautiful, charming place to him, and all he could do was look like a thundercloud, refuse to play nice, get her all hot and bothered, and then somehow fail to know one darn thing about who she was or what she liked. World peace. Mother Teresa. There was nothing wrong with those things, but...he had made her sound like some stupid Miss America candidate. And she hated Miss America candidates.

"Creepy," he said. "I haven't put my finger on it yet. But there's something wrong here."

Zoë shook her head. "It's just honeymoony. A little cheesy maybe, but you know what? Nothing wrong with that, either."

She rose from the bed, waiting for him to clear the stairs. When he stayed where he was, blocking the way, she squeezed past him anyway, pretending she didn't care how close he was or how nice he smelled.

Safely down in the living room again, Zoë grabbed the whole basket of fruit and snacks, determined to enjoy the place and all its charms. She put in a CD, choosing Sarah McLachlan from the choices on the shelf, then dropped into the leather chair, put her feet up on the ottoman, and polished off all the strawberries *and* the bread and cheese. Feeling very righteous, she thought it was pretty amusing she hadn't asked Jake if he wanted any. Ha! Take that. She could be just as selfish and annoying as he was.

From the loft upstairs, leaning over the railing to yell down into the living room, Jake suddenly demanded, "Where is all of our stuff?"

"Huh?"

He came hammering down the stairs. "They said they would have our luggage here, ready for us. Well, some of it is unpacked and put away in the dresser and in the bathroom. My badge is here and my toothbrush, but not my notebook or my clothes or my cell phone or even my wallet. There's a note," he said, holding it up in one hand, "to inform us that all other personal items are being held in a locker at the Lodge and we can't get them until we check out."

"And this upsets you because...?" Zoë popped another grape into her mouth, ignoring him.

"Because I don't like them pawing through my stuff and deciding what I can keep and what I can't. I don't like them telling me what to wear and taking away my clothes." He started pacing in between her and Sarah McLachlan, and interfering with her serenity.

"I'm sure they'll give it back to you if you ask."

"Nope. It says on this note that you can't have it back, so don't ask. Like I said," he went on, "this place is creepy. Captain Picard was creepy. His minions were creepy. That exercise he wanted us to do was creepy. Ron and Tori and the other Stepford couples were creepy."

"Captain Picard, huh? I was thinking Mr. Clean." He didn't respond. "Okay, okay, I get it." Stretching, Zoë lifted herself from the chair, deciding to do a little check of her own. It took about three seconds to go up, look through the dresser and closet, give the bathroom a glance and pop back down. "The only thing I cared about, which is my personal item, is safe and accounted for."

"You mean that stupid pink card with the swans on it."

"Yes, well...yes." She hadn't realized he knew about the tarot card. "But my toothbrush, a few cosmetics, my hairbrush and hairpins and scunchies, even my underwear. All here."

There was a funny look in his eyes when he said, "Yeah, I saw the undies."

Which was worse? Camp personnel poking through her lingerie? Or Jake? "That's something you didn't have to worry about," she noted tartly, "since you don't wear any."

His brows lowered. "One more thing you know about me and I don't know how you know it."

"Well, there's a perfectly reasonable explanation. I saw. You, I mean. In the, uh, dressing room. Sorry. But you do have, you know, a wonderful bottom," she said hastily, and then wished she hadn't. "One of the all-time great bottoms." Okay, this was just getting worse. She retreated to a better choice. "You're right, that the rest of my clothes and shoes are gone. But I'm not worried. The bathroom is stocked with nifty products, every kind of cream and lotion and soap you could want. I tried some of the body lotion. Very nice." She sniffed her hand. "Smells like coconut and pineapple. What's not to like? And the closet and drawers are full of more pants and tops like these, plus socks and robes and slippers and even bathing suits. Okay, so it all has the EJ logo. Don't you think they're just pushing their products?"

"I think it's a cult."

"A cult. First prison and now a cult." Zoë rolled her eyes, hoping he was watching her show of disdain. "I think it's great they provide so much. And did you see the kitchen? Juice, crackers, cookies, chocolate, marshmallows. Everything we need."

"Speaking of everything we need, you must've missed the boatload of condoms next to the bed," he said in the most sarcastic tone she'd ever heard. "Plus more in the bathroom. An invitation to go crazy, kids."

She got the idea he was a little miffed she hadn't risen

to his bait about the underwear, so he was upping the ante. But she could feel her face growing hotter. She had not missed the "boatload" of condoms. Or the somewhat exotic powder, gel and set of edible body paints next to the condom jar, all of which promised sensual delights for creative couples. She'd just preferred not to mention any of that. "The place is crawling with honeymooners. Of course condoms make sense. Although the fact that none of ours get used might make Housekeeping suspicious."

"Forget the condoms," Jake returned impatiently.

"Happily." Liar, liar, pants on fire. There was no way she could forget them or not think about what everyone else in this damn place was doing with them. *And* the body paints.

But Jake was on to a new topic. "There's no phone in the place, did you notice? Not even a phone jack."

"So people are into seclusion and privacy and no interruptions while they..." She broke off and then finished up, "You know, do whatever it is they're all doing, even as we speak. I still don't see what the problem is."

But Jake wasn't listening. He was prowling around, apparently looking for phone jacks. And then he pushed a red button set into the wall near the door.

Immediately a pleasant voice coming from the direction of the button inquired, "Did you need something, Mr. Calhoun? Mrs. Calhoun? Did you want to order some dinner? More pillows? Towels? Condoms? Extra EJ products?"

Jake mumbled, "Uh, no thanks."

Zoë was still back on the fact that someone had just called her Mrs. Calhoun, even if it was a disembodied voice.

"See what I mean?" Jake turned back to her. "No

phone, just an intercom. This place is beyond weird. There is something very wrong here." He squinted into the corners of the room, looking around very intently, and then he started to unscrew the lampshade.

"What are you doing?"

"Looking for bugs and cameras."

"Bugs and...? Okay, now you've gone off the deep end." Was he doing this just to avoid speaking to or looking at *her?* Was this more avoidance? That was her best guess.

Snagging a three-ring binder that said "For Our Guests" on the outside, Zoë settled back in the comfy chair and began leafing through the notebook. "Why, look!" she announced in her most studiously perky voice, just to annoy him. "The schedule is in here. And room-service information. We can order any food on the menu delivered right to our door twenty-four hours a day. Including the gigantic Honeymooners Banana Split that comes with ice cream scoops and three jars of toppings, nuts, maraschino cherries, and...special vinyl covering for the bed? What the...?"

But then she thought about it. *Honeymooners* banana split. In bed. For two. She squeezed her eyes shut, but that didn't stop the image of Jake piling ice cream and hot fudge on her naked body, with a cherry on top. "Oh, my God," she whispered.

As her upper lip began to perspire, she decided she was really sorry she'd brought that up. Luckily Jake was too into casing the joint for bugs and video equipment to have heard her.

Lifting her hair with one weak hand, she turned the page, away from room service and on to Explorer's Journey products. "It says we're encouraged to use all the EJ lotions and shampoo and soaps we want, and wear all these clothes, at no extra cost. We even get to take them home with us. All included. What a great program, huh?"

Jake was standing center of the room, staring up at the skylight. "This is a very weird place, and they're hiding something."

She slammed down the three-ring binder, making a satisfying smack on the coffee table. She was so tired of his avoidance. "They're not hiding anything. But you are."

A long pause hung in the air. "I am? And how about you?"

Zoë sat up straighter as Jake advanced on her. "What do you mean?" she asked. "I'm not hiding anything." Except maybe the fact that she now wanted nothing more from life than to eat ice cream off his bare stomach and she couldn't bring herself to admit it. But that was hardly earth-shattering.

"Are you telling me everything, Zoë?" He bent down, braced his hands on the arms of the chair and leaned in over her. Squashing herself as far into the leather chair as she could get, she tilted her head back and stared right up into his face.

He smelled like the Explorer's Journey lotion she'd smoothed into her arms and neck. Had he used some, too? Why did every glimpse of him, every whiff of him, make her fixate on the fact that he looked good enough to eat? What was wrong with her?

"Did you use some of the EJ lotion?" she asked. Mmm...she breathed it in. Coconut, pineapple, maybe banana. Banana split...with Jake underneath...

"No," he snapped. "I used the soap. Why?"

She widened her eyes, trying to concentrate. "No reason."

"You are not going to put me off with this junk about how much you like their free stuff," he said angrily. "I'm trying to get to what's really going on here. No more about the soap or the powder or any other magic potions, okay?"

"Okay, okay."

"So let's start with the fact that you seem to lie very easily," he continued in the same dark and unamused tone. "I already know you're more than happy to fake a whole honeymoon on the spur of the moment for no particular reason. Is there anything else I don't know about?"

Visions of her pretty pink True Love card danced in her head. What would he do if he knew she'd only come on this trip because she thought she'd gotten a cosmic kick in the pants from a tarot card? "I—I don't lie. I'm really a very honest person," she assured him.

"Uh-huh. Which is why you had such fun making up that whole story about us being married—twice—for that lady on the bus. I'm surprised you didn't give us three or four children."

"Don't you think we're a little young for four kids to be credible?" she tried.

He didn't move, dipping even closer, and she began to feel very uncomfortable with him hovering over her like this, with his warm breath dusting her nose, with his heady coco-banana scent invading her nose and making her want to eat him up with a spoon. At the moment, they weren't touching anywhere, but it was almost worse like this, with him so close and her so trapped, but *not* touching.

Jake tipped his head to one side. "I also liked all the lies you were shoveling about having a bunch of jobs, to cover the fact that I didn't know what you did for a living."

"That was true," she protested. "I mean, you were wrong about me being a professional psychic. It's too funny you thought that." She managed a hollow laugh for his benefit. "The tarot cards are just for me, and I'm really not any good at it. So that is not one of my jobs. But I do have a bunch of jobs. Just...not that."

"And one is teaching seniors how to dance?"

"Yes," she swore. "Really. More like lead the class, really. As opposed to teaching. Dance is very good for them and has been shown to have healing powers."

When he didn't say anything, just seemed to be judging and weighing her words, she went on, "I also waitress at a breakfast place. The Bonjour Café. That's good because I make good tips and I'm done by noon. Plus I work part-time in the box office at Steppenwolf, and I usher at Second City and the Shakespeare Theatre at Navy Pier, none of which pays very well, but I can eat at the Bonjour Café and see the plays for free. So, you know, eating and theater. Who needs more?"

"Which explains the 'Lead on, MacSlug' thing."

"Macduff," she corrected. "It's 'Lead on, Macduff.'"

"I remember." His eyes were hooded and his jaw was clenched so tight she was afraid he was going to start spitting out teeth. "But that doesn't explain how you knew my name before I told you. Or how you had all the right answers to the questions about me. My favorite food, who my hero is, what I most value in life...how the hell did you know that?"

"Well, I..."

She swallowed, gazing up into his rigid features. He wasn't going to like whatever explanation she gave him, was he? The reality was, she didn't know how she knew.

She just looked at Jake and all these bits of info flooded her brain. He liked Wheaties. He liked driving really, really fast. He hated to fish but loved hanging out with his brothers, so he pretended. She hadn't a clue about a lot of other things, but she knew without asking that he was looking for a woman in sparkly shoes because his father wanted him to.

And he was more mad at himself for being sexually frustrated than he was with her for not leveling with him.

How funny. She hadn't realized that till right this minute. Zoë's lips parted. Jake wanted her. He wanted her bad. And it was making him cranky.

"Damn it, Zoë, tell me," he growled. "I need the truth."

"I can explain," she murmured, thinking more about how nice his lips were and how wonderful he smelled. "But if you could... You're kind of scaring me."

Swearing under his breath, Jake backed off, and she thought for a second or two that he was giving in, giving up, letting her off the hook, giving her a chance to breathe. But he suddenly turned, he picked up both her feet, and in a move that came out of nowhere, he yanked off her sneakers, stripped off her socks, and threw both socks and shoes onto the rug behind him.

"What are you doing?" she squealed, so surprised she didn't even try to pull away.

Holding a bare foot securely in each hand, Jake frowned as he scrutinized them. "I don't know. I can't tell anything anymore." His gaze lifted, meeting hers. "Tell me the truth," he demanded. "Are you Toni?"

8

ZOË GLANCED at her toes, back up at him, back at her toes, and then it dawned. "Oh...feet. Her." She tugged away from his grasp, forcing him to let go. "Good grief, Jake, of course not! Why would I be her?"

"But how do you know the things you know?"

"So you think Toni might know those things, and therefore since I knew, I might be Toni." She considered that for a moment. It made a certain amount of sense, but it was also complicated and made her head hurt. That and the fact that she kept smelling the coconut and pineapple aroma, which made her obsess about covering Jake with ice cream and chocolate sauce. It was no wonder she was having a hard time.

"So?" he prompted.

"What? I already told you I'm not Toni," she declared. "Do you want ID?"

"I already know you don't have ID, because the EJ guards stole it all," he returned indignantly. "Besides, if you were Toni the con woman, you could have more IDs in more names than the driver's license bureau."

Con woman? Sheesh. He had even a shred of suspicion that *she* was a con woman?

She raised her right hand. "My name is Zoë Elizabeth Kidd. My name has always been Zoë Elizabeth Kidd, and I have never gone by any other name. I do not believe I have even known a woman named Toni, and especially not one with sparkly plastic shoes. I am an incredibly trustworthy person. Everyone who knows me says that about me. Would you like references? Or do you believe me?"

"Maybe." He frowned. "I still want to know how you know the things you do."

She shrugged. No way, in his current mood, was she going to try to explain this sudden—and really inexplicable—surge of psychic powers. He was such a skeptic. Besides, except for the tarot cards and a tiny bit of intuition here and there, she'd never experienced this before herself. Raising her chin, she told him, "I'm a good judge of character."

His gaze was steady and uncompromising. "I thought maybe you'd tell me you were psychic or something."

"You don't believe in psychics."

"No, I don't."

"So I guess I can't be one then, can I?" she inquired coolly.

"No one is psychic, Zoë. I just thought that might be your excuse, your way of getting around the truth."

Well, that was insulting. Fuming at his attitude, she jumped up from her chair and retrieved her shoes and socks.

Had she thought Jake's appearance in her life was a cosmic kick in the pants? How about a cosmic joke? She couldn't believe that any higher power would ever have intended that *he* could be her true love. He was snotty and mean and suspicious and *so* pushy. How aggravating that she just wanted to enjoy her fruit-and-cheese basket and try out the fun soaps and lotions, maybe order a little room service, and he was such a downer. What in the world had he been thinking, grabbing and exposing her feet like that? She thought she had perfectly nice feet. Not con woman's feet at all.

And why was he so gorgeous? Another cosmic joke. What was up with that? Why waste that beautiful exterior on a cynical control freak like Jake?

Meanwhile, he was circling again, getting closer, close enough for her to catch his scent. She certainly didn't need to inhale him and start thinking dangerous thoughts again.

Still clutching her socks and sneakers, she held him off with both hands. "No more interrogations. You don't need to take out your frustrations on me. Frustrations in the sense of the search for Toni not going so well," she added hastily. "That's all. No other kind of, you know, frustration."

"You still haven't given any explanation for how you know all these things, Zoë. Like my name. My favorite food. About my dad."

"I just figured it out. Look," she pointed out, "you knew my favorite food was strawberries. How did *you* know?"

"Well, I..." Was he blushing? How very curious. Now she really wanted to know the answer. He mumbled, "Just a guess."

"There you go. So I made educated guesses, too. We talked in the car on the way to the airport, remember?" she said, moving a little closer, warming to the topic now that she was making headway. "People always say feminine intuition, blah blah blah. Well, here's a news flash. It's based on paying attention. On actually listening. Women do a much better job of that than men, so men pretend it's all a fluke. Intuition. Ha!"

"There's no need to get—"

"Oh, yes, there is," she went on, riding roughshod

over his words. "You see, I already knew you were a cop, plus you told me about your family and being on the force. It was a foregone conclusion that you would be into loyalty and doing right by people. It's written all over you. Stand-up guy, always does the right thing, hates disappointing people, rock, anchor, all that."

"That doesn't explain my—"

She waved that objection off, too, interrupting, "I bet ninety percent of men pick their fathers as their heroes. It's just logical."

It took him a moment, but finally he offered a grudging "Okay, I guess I can accept that."

She was pretty pleased to be showing off her deductive reasoning and getting the best of him in this discussion. Advancing on *him* for once, going toe-to-toe, tapping the tip of one shoe into his hard chest, she announced, "I will even go you one further, Jake. I will demonstrate the power of my logic. Even though you won't tell me why you're here, I'll bet this has to do with your father, right?"

She couldn't read his expression, but she already knew she was on the money. Just as well as she knew her own name and his taste in Wheaties, she was certain she was right. "That's why you're so determined to find this Toni con woman. Because she either conned or attempted to con your dad, the man you respect most in the world, he asked you to find her, and you would do anything, even go on a bogus honeymoon with an annoying woman who quotes Shakespeare, rather than let him down."

No comment.

"I can tell from your face I'm right," she concluded.

"I don't think you're that annoying," he said softly,

staring down at her. "And if you really can tell all that from my face, you'd have made one hell of a detective."

"I'm not that annoying?" she echoed, searching his eyes. That was practically a declaration of love coming from him.

Sure, watch him change tactics and get nice all of a sudden just to keep her off balance. He was like good cop/bad cop all in one package. He was infuriating. He was also adorable.

God, she wanted him to kiss her. Who was she kidding? Kiss her? She wanted him to peel off her clothes and make love to her for about a hundred years on that silly round bed under the jungle vines. She wanted to get on the horn to room service and get that Honeymooners Banana Split here in three minutes or less.

How long ago had it been since she'd mocked him by telling him she would have no problem keeping her hands off? Ten minutes? Maybe twenty? Dropping her gaze, she stared down at her hands, hanging on to those shoes for dear life, just to keep them occupied. Hands off? Oh, man, this was impossible.

Are you afraid the big, bad, round Tarzan bed is going to suck you in? Or I'm going to jump you and throw you on it? I'm not the one who kissed you, am I? I'm not the one who got all stoked up during the serenity exercise.

Liar, liar. They were both sizzling with sexual frustration, and he wasn't the only one who was cranky. This cottage was just way too small. And Jake was standing way too close.

But he thought I could be a con woman. He still thinks I'm lying. She couldn't be this attracted to someone who didn't trust her, could she?

Finally he broke the silence. He reached over, slid one finger under her chin and tipped it up, so that she had to look at him again, eye-to-eye. "Why did you pick me as your hero?"

That came out of left field. "I—I don't know."

"Your hero, Zoë," he repeated. "You must've written it down on your paper for some reason."

"I don't know. It's hard to explain."

"Try."

Reluctantly she tried to come up with her reasoning. It was so difficult with his eyes on her. "I just think, if I really was married to someone like you, someone who puts his life on the line for other people every single day, someone I knew I could depend on every single day, to always do the right thing, that of course you would be my hero."

She lifted her shoulders in a self-conscious shrug. She wanted to wrap her arms around him. She wanted to feel his strength and his heat and the power of his embrace. He really was such a stand-up guy, and there was something very appealing about that, after a lifetime of being let down.

But he wasn't hers to depend on, was he?

"I'm sorry, Jake," she said, edging away, far enough that his finger was no longer brushing her chin. "I'm sorry if that puts you on the spot. It just seemed like the right answer at the time, while I was pretending you were mine. I'm sorry."

He nodded quickly and moved off, over near the fireplace, far enough that she could breathe again. He played with the switch that turned the flames up and down, finally choosing to turn the fireplace off altogether.

After a moment, he said, "So, did you say there was a schedule in that book?"

"Yeah."

"What's up for tomorrow?" he asked gruffly. "Should I plan ahead? Maybe quiz you before we do it so I don't look so stupid this time?"

Phew. A safe and neutral topic. "Well, there was couples meditation, like we did today." Which had hardly turned out either safe or neutral. She hurried to add, "And confession session, whatever that is. I think I also saw something about a balancing exercise, like a balance beam, maybe? I'm not sure, but I think they want to explore trust."

"Balancing? Okay." He rubbed his hands together. "You're a dancer, plus you do yoga, right? You must be good at balance. Excellent. We can kill on that one. Ron and Tori will be dead meat."

Dead meat? Kill? Trust Jake to frame a trust exercise in terms of bodily harm. More evidence that there was no way he could be her true love. She decided not to tell him she was terrible at yoga, either. "Jake, I think you're a little too competitive. This isn't about winning," she told him. "It's about trying to be a better person, knowing yourself and your partner, understanding and helping each other, you know?"

"You already seem to understand me pretty well. And I'd say you are pretty highly evolved in general," he said lightly, his tone letting her know he was using words like "highly evolved" for her benefit. "Think you still need to work on yourself, huh?"

"Are you kidding? That's the whole reason I wanted to come." Well, not the whole reason. There was a small matter of the True Love card.

"To work on yourself?" he asked. "I don't get it. What do you need to improve?"

"It's very kind of you to say that, but I need some focus. I need to know where I'm going," she explained, trying not to sound too defensive about it. "I told you about my sad and pathetic patchwork of jobs."

Jake wrinkled his brow. "I didn't think it sounded sad or pathetic. You said you were helping people with the dancing, and with the other jobs, you had food and theater, and that was all you needed."

"I was putting a positive spin on it." She sat back in the chair and pulled on her socks, realizing here was yet another place where they didn't match up. He was defined by his career and his family, and she had neither. He seemed so sure of his direction, and she was wandering in the wilderness.

"But if you like what you do, isn't that all that's important?" he asked, still looking confused.

Zoë tied her shoes up tight. "Waitress, usher, dance teacher. Don't you think it's maybe time I figured out what I want to be when I grow up? It's easy for you—you always knew you would be a cop."

"Did I?" He shrugged. "Maybe."

"And it's more than that, anyway. The Explorer's Journey, I mean. It's about...about growing as a couple."

Gently he reminded her, "But we're not a couple."

"I know." Even though he was totally the wrong man for her, even though his presence in her life was a cosmic joke, she couldn't help but feel more than a twinge of regret. "That's a problem."

But his eyes held her. Speculative, sweet, tempting...so very blue.

Given the look on his face right now, the warm feeling that continued to hum through her veins as she basked in the glow of that heated gaze, it was a problem she thought she was actually making progress on.

Oh, no. Logic told her he was not the one for her. But her heart was telling her something else again.

"Zoë..."

"Yes?"

"I'm sorry," he said awkwardly, "about the empathy test. I'm sorry I didn't ask what you did for a living or any of the rest of it. If we're going to keep up the pretense, I guess I should do a better job, huh?"

Zoë smiled, feeling all her objections soften, warm, melt. Wow. Maybe she was making more progress than she thought. Jake had apologized. He wanted to know more about her. Resolute Jake was unbending. "Jake, would you maybe want to look at the menu and see if you want to order some dinner? I'm kind of—" she licked her lips "—hungry."

"You already ate everything in that basket. And you're so small. How can you still be hungry?" Pulling his gaze away, shaking his head, he picked up the binder and started flipping pages. "How about a big, greasy cheeseburger?"

"Not on the menu. But there's a tofu burger. I saw it."

His head jerked up. "You're kidding, right?"

"No. No red meat. It's in their philosophy on the first page of the book." She crossed over behind him. "See? Page one?"

"I'm supposed to last a week without meat?"

"You'll do fine, Jake. Just try it, okay?" Before he could say no, she strode over to the intercom and pushed the button. As soon as the disembodied voice answered, Zoë ordered two tofu cheeseburgers, fries and some beer.

"I didn't say I wanted beer."

"Jake, Jake, Jake," she teased. "We're in Wisconsin. Gotta have beer."

His lips curved into a delicious smile, and once again, she had to clamp down hard to keep herself from swooning at his feet or offering to vault over the electric fence to go out in the real world and find him a meat cheeseburger. She had this penchant for volunteering to help.

"You don't seem like the beer type," he noted dryly.

"Yeah, well, you're not the tofu type, either. What can I say?" She grinned, feeling bizarrely light-headed, weirdly happy. "You know, Jake, marriage is all about compromise."

THE TOFU BURGER was one of the worst things he'd ever eaten in his life. And he kept his mouth shut about it. He had decided that this program was all about the team concept, and he figured he was taking a tofu burger for the team.

Zoë chomped away on hers, and he sneaked a few fries off her plate, enjoying the enthusiasm with which she approached even something as disgusting as a tofu burger. True, she was a flake, but she was also the sweetest, nicest, most genuine woman he had ever met.

She was also a hottie, but he was choosing to ignore that. As best he could.

Jake frowned. Life was a lot easier when he was still planning to bolt at the earliest opportunity, to go over the wall ASAP. But after sharing a dressing room, breathing exercises, empathy tests, tofu burgers, and some very entertaining conversation with Zoë, he knew he couldn't just walk out.

He remembered the look on her face when she'd read her greatest fear off that piece of paper. *Watching the love of my life walk away…*

While Jake was under no illusion that that referred to him—it had to be that Wylie guy—he still had some trouble contemplating waltzing off into the sunset and leaving her here by herself. She was so excited about the confession sessions and the balance beam and really wanted to gain something from this utterly stupid program, and she couldn't do it by herself. If he still felt bad for humiliating her by screwing up the empathy exam, how could he leave and let all these other people think her new husband dumped her?

No. It wasn't in him to leave and let Zoë down that way. All in all, he guessed he was staying, at least for now.

As they ate, the sun had dipped in the sky, providing a great sunset, as promised, and every time he looked at Zoë across the table, she had a streaky orange-and-pink glow behind her head. She was already pretty enough. She didn't need the halo.

He swigged the last of his beer, washing down any remaining taste of that awful fake burger. He'd had his beer and hers both, after she took two sips and decided she didn't want it. "So," he began, putting the empty bottle aside. "What's for dessert?"

Suddenly her cheeks were as pink as the sunset. "Well, there's this banana split thing on the room service menu," she stammered. "You're supposed to... I mean, they think you will...but you don't have to."

He raised an eyebrow. She had this funny spark in her eyes, and her whole face was flushed with color. Over ice cream? Only Zoë would blush over a banana split. "I think there's stuff for s'mores in there," he suggested tactfully. "Why don't we do that instead?"

"I don't know what that is," she told him.

Now it was his turn to be surprised. "S'mores. You toast marshmallows, like on a stick, over a campfire, and then you squash them between chocolate bars and graham crackers, to melt the chocolate. It was all laid out on the counter in there, and I'm sure they had s'mores in mind. What, you never went camping when you were a kid? Girl Scouts? Brownies? Not even computer camp?"

"No. Well, I..." She gave him a funny look. "Is this s'mores thing something everyone knows about?"

"I don't know. I never thought about it."

"Well, I never heard of them." She rose from the table, clearing away the dishes and bottles and neatly stacking them inside the square wooden basket they'd arrived in. Busying herself with napkins and utensils, she mumbled, "I had kind of a weird childhood."

"City girl, huh?"

"Not exactly." She was so quiet he was a little taken aback. Ask her about dancing or Shakespeare or even the wonders of meditation, and she got all bubbly and effusive. Mention childhood and suddenly she was shy. "But, you know, those s'mores things don't sound very good, anyway, so I don't think we need to make them. Can't we just eat the chocolate?"

"Sure. It's kind of hot to build a fire, anyway." He slid open the door to let her and the tray pass through, back into the air-conditioned cabin. But he couldn't let it go. "So what was weird about your childhood?"

"I shouldn't have said that. It wasn't weird. No camp. But I'm sure a lot of kids don't go to camp."

"Uh-huh. You're an only child, right?" He waited. If he gave Zoë enough time, he knew she would come out with it.

And she did. "My parents are very different—from each other, I mean." She frowned. "It's not a big deal. Really. My mom's great, kind of counterculture, an artist in San Francisco. She does mosaics. Beautiful mosaics. She's very talented. And my dad's great, too, but he's the total opposite. He works for the State Department.

You would look at these people and think, how did they ever get together?"

"Opposites attract?" he tried.

"But they probably shouldn't," she said curtly. "Not if my parents are any indication. They split when I was one, thank goodness, because they really can't stand each other. I lived with my mom in San Francisco, which was really cool. Unstructured, but cool. As for my dad...I spent my summers with him in D.C. for a while, which meant I actually spent my summers with his housekeeper."

Jake was starting to feel he was way over his head. What were you supposed to say when someone told you her childhood was a mess? Was "sorry" enough? He took a different tack. "So you said he works for the State Department? What does he do?"

"I don't know, exactly. I never did." She laughed. "I keep expecting him to be outed as a Russian spy, you know?"

"You think your father is a spy?" he asked slowly. What in the world was she talking about? Every time he thought he had Zoë figured out, there was a new layer. Mom an artist and Dad a *spy?*

"No, no. Not really," she assured him. "I just thought about it when I was a kid. Like one day I would open the newspaper and it would say, 'Richard Kidd, career diplomat, discovered to be a spy for the Russians.' 'We never knew him,' say neighbors. 'Me, neither,' says his daughter.'"

If he were a different person, he would've suggested she had abandonment issues. The missing dad, the missing fiancé, her greatest fear. He knew about that stuff from psych courses he'd taken in college. But he preferred to deal with the here and the now instead of worrying about childhood scars. His philosophy was, you went on and you got past it. No wallowing.

Still, he felt bad for Zoë.

"What are you looking so glum about?" she joked, giving him a poke in the ribs. "Snap out of it. So I never had a s'more. Like I said, they sound pretty vile to me, anyway. I'll live."

"I gotta tell you, I don't think you missed anything. I never liked them that much, either. Too sweet. You always burn your mouth on the marshmallow, and the chocolate doesn't melt right."

She beamed at him. "Thanks for the loyalty, Jake. You are really wonderful, you know that?"

Zoë didn't ask for much, did she? Skip s'mores and she was your friend for life. Jake shook his head. How had he never met anyone like her before?

He glanced around the small cabin, once more aware of just how small it was. Although it was dark outside by now, he was wide awake. And he definitely needed something to do to get his mind off how small the place was and how tempting the company. "So, what do you want to do?" he asked heartily. "Watch TV? Are there any games or cards in here?"

"I don't see any games." She switched on the television, but there was only snow no matter what channel she chose. "Well, there are all kinds of DVDs. Why don't you pick a movie, and I'll go take a shower? I'm feeling kind of buggy after being outside."

As she hopped up the stairs to the loft, he ambled over and took a look at the shelf of DVDs. Oh, great. The first one he pulled out was *Kama Sutra Secrets*, with naked people, their skin glistening, twisted like pretzels into at least three positions he'd never seen before—and that was just the cover. He turned the thing about forty-five degrees, squinting at it. "How in the hell do you do that?"

He looked at the other choices. *Advanced Kama Sutra Secrets. Tantric Sex to Blow Your Mind. Hot Chakra. The Big O. Even Bigger O. The Biggest O.* Plus *Body Heat, 9 1/2 Weeks, Last Tango in Paris*, and titles that only went downhill from there.

"Talk about one-track minds," he growled, slamming *Kama Sutra Secrets* back on the shelf before the cover burned his hand. He'd knocked over dirty bookstores with tamer stuff than this.

Quickly he made sure none of the pictures were turned out and the shelf looked neat before Zoë came back. His mind might be branded with images of people boinking upside down and backward, but he didn't want her to see them. He could still hear the water running upstairs, and Zoë singing to herself.

"Could've guessed that one," he muttered. Of course she sang in the shower. He couldn't tell what the song was, but he'd have bet his bottom dollar it was something about the sun coming out tomorrow.

Sunshine and lollipops upstairs and hot chakras downstairs. No wonder he was a mess.

The water stopped. The door to the bathroom upstairs opened, and the scent of fruit salad wafted down the stairs. Zoë came tripping down not long after, barefoot, smiling, still wet, wrapped in a fluffy white robe that had EJ embroidered on the chest.

He could hear the song now, but it wasn't about sunbeams. What was she crooning? Something about "sssteam"? What the hell?

"What are you singing?" he demanded.

"'Steam Heat,'" she said happily. "It's from *The Pajama Game*. Good song, huh?"

"No. I thought..." But what difference did it make what he'd thought? Like everything else in this damn place, she was focused on heat and steam, on stoking the boiler, on turning up the temperature. Yeah, well, he needed the temp to drop a few degrees. Pronto.

As Zoë neared the bottom step, Jake was overcome with the strangest sensations. He would never have picked himself as the type to go for a girl who smelled like a banana smoothie, but he had to admit, on her it was really enticing. More than enticing. It was overwhelming and...amazing. In an instant, he was dying to touch her and run his hands inside her robe, to press his lips to her pineapple-and-coconut-scented skin. He wanted to taste her. Every inch of her.

Whoa. Where did that come from?

"Did you find a movie?" she asked innocently.

"Uh, no. Nothing good."

"Really?" She walked over to the cabinets flanking the TV. "Nothing?"

"Zoë, don't look at those." He inserted himself in between her and the bookshelves before she had a chance to pick anything up. Bad idea. That tantalizing aroma just kept filling his nostrils and he couldn't think straight. He was one big hunk of burning love.

Good Lord. He'd only had two beers! Backing up in a hurry, he stumbled over the edge of the white shag rug.

"Are you okay?" she asked, looking puzzled.

"Yeah, fine. It's just..." He had to get out of there. He had to get away from her. "I got really tired all of a sudden. I think maybe I should go to bed now."

"Oh." Her eyebrows rose. "Okay. Where do you want to...?" She crooked her thumb at the stairs to the loft.

"Upstairs? Did we ever settle what we were going to do?"

"No, no. But I'll just...the hammock."

He was out of there like a shot.

9

IT WAS MUGGY and buggy and he could hear crickets and birds and all manner of animals likely to keep him up for hours. He didn't care. He sank into the hammock, prepared to be in pain all night. The thing wasn't as easy to get into as it looked, and it started to rock and wobble as he eased himself in. The woven strings were also not very comfortable, biting into his skin through the soft fabric of the tracksuit. And then something bit him on the cheek. He slapped himself, missing it completely.

Scree...the door to the cabin slid open.

Zoë stood framed in the light from inside. "Jake, that doesn't look comfortable at all. You look all squashed and miserable and your bottom is about an inch from the ground. That can't be right."

He tried to turn over far enough to talk to her, almost falling right out the side of the damn thing. He hung on with everything he had. "It doesn't matter," he said tersely. "I'm sleeping here."

"That's really stupid," she argued. "This was my trip and my responsibility and I'm smaller and I should be the one to sleep in the hammock."

"Zoë, that's crazy—"

"If you won't get out, I'll just come in, too."

"Zoë, don't even try that."

But she ignored him, grasping the banded edge, pushing down so she could roll in. Unfortunately, all she did was knock the whole thing completely out of whack, tipping him out and knocking her off her feet. Both went sprawling. When he hit the ground, he caught her in the shin, she made an "oof" sound and tumbled over right on top of him, bracing herself with both arms on his chest.

Jeez. Not only were their approximate body positions very close to one of the choices on the back of the Kama Sutra video, but her robe had gaped open, putting his eyes right on a level with her cleavage. Fresh from the shower, she wasn't wearing anything under the robe. She smelled so good, so incredibly good, practically a cloud of that maddening scent, and her skin was unbelievably soft when he tried to pull her lapels back together, tried to gingerly, carefully, tug the robe back around her hips so it would meet in the middle.

He snatched his hands away, holding them clear, but it was too late. He'd already seen the pale curve of her breast, the slope of her shoulder, and felt the silky smoothness of her thigh where she straddled him. Nothing more than provocative glimpses in the moonlight, fleeting contact in the still, hot night, and yet it was worse than seeing and touching everything. Much worse. This was like an appetizer, imprinting Zoë on his libido even more strongly than before, making him want her even more. But not getting anything close to what he needed.

As he pushed himself away and she tipped back, safely under her own power, his hands clenched and he swore under his breath. Here he was, responsible Jake Calhoun, acting like a walking erection, a blazing streak of sex. Out of control. Completely out of control.

"Are you trying to torture me?" he demanded. "Because you are doing one hell of a job."

A little wobbly, she stood up, securely fastening her
robe around her. "You never should've been out here in
the first place." She swatted at some insect flying by.
"What's wrong with you? You could get a tick and get
Lyme disease. Or Rocky Mountain spotted fever. Or
West Nile virus."

"Okay, okay." Another bug buzzed his ear and he
slashed a hand at it. He knew when he was beat. He was
also desperate for some sleep, some relief, at this point.
If he stayed out here, all he would be doing was replay-
ing the hammock action all night. "There's a bathtub in
the basement. I'll sleep there. Or the chair in the living
room. It has an ottoman."

"You've got to be kidding," she protested. "Have you
seen the size of that stupid bed? We could fit both of us,
Tarzan, *and* a few apes, and still not have any body parts
touching."

Wearily he murmured, "Zoë, we can't. I can't."

"Oh, yes, you can!" she snapped. "I am not going to
let you sleep on the deck or in the bathtub or in a chair.
You wouldn't get any sleep, you'd be all cranky and
creaky in the morning, you'll fall off the balance beam
and we'll get our butts kicked by Ron and Tori, and I'm
not dealing with that! So there."

He stood there, stubborn. "No. The two of us in the
bed—it just wouldn't work."

But Zoë wasn't budging, either. "We are adults, Jake.
We've both acknowledged that there is a certain attraction thing going on here. We said we wouldn't do anything, and we won't."

She opened the door to the cottage, waiting for him to
go in first. He said nothing, trying to decide what to do.

"Jake, I swear I will not touch you. And I trust you.
Sheesh. Remember who you are. You're the truest of the

True Blue Calhouns." She rolled her eyes. "Look at what just happened. I mean, all the right pieces were kind of, you know, *lined up* there for a sec. Something could have happened. For a lot of people, it would have. Did anything happen? No! Why not? Because you, of all the people in the known universe, would never lose control. Not out here and not up there."

How nice that she had so much faith in him. Now if only he shared it. "Are you sure?"

"Jake, just get in here," she shot back, clearly beyond her patience with him.

He followed her inside, immediately welcoming the cooler air. It had to be better in here, didn't it? And she was right about one thing—you didn't need a bed to make love. You didn't need a bed to be very, very turned-on or very, very strained. Bed or no, he could control himself, couldn't he?

Upstairs they went, him lagging behind a few paces. Zoë immediately grabbed some things out of the stock in the chest of drawers, retreating into the bathroom and then returning wearing an oversize EJ T-shirt and a pair of drawstring pants. She'd braided her hair, she had no makeup on, and she looked about sixteen. And he still wanted her more than he had ever wanted anything in his life.

"Look," she announced, throwing out her arms. "Perfectly respectable. Nonthreatening. If you want me to wrap myself in the big ol' honkin' terry-cloth robe before I get in the bed, I can do that, too."

He didn't look at her. He couldn't. "Not necessary." He already knew the robe wasn't enough protection, no matter how thick the fabric. "I'm going to take a shower. If you could just, uh, go ahead and get in, that would be a big help."

She nodded, edging around him and the wide curve at the end of the huge bed, ducking under the jungle vines to slip in on the far side. As he stood there for a moment, he could hear her punching the pillow, rustling around in the sheets. Practically vaulting into the shower, he turned it all the way to cold. Freezing cold. And he took the soap out of the tray and dropped it in the wastebasket, not sure he could take another whiff of that maddening banana and coconut. Plain old water was fine, thanks.

He stayed in there as long as he could, but he really was exhausted, and he finally had to come out. Cold and wet, he was a lot more rational.

Darkness. Silence. Good.

He searched the drawers and found a pair of EJ-logo shorts, backed into the corner, dropped his towel and slid on the shorts. Listening for sounds from her side of the bed, he maneuvered himself in, poking his head between the leaves, putting one knee down, slowly easing under the sheets.

And then he lay there, immobile, not moving a muscle. The curtain of silk vines made it very dark in there. And the size of the bed was deceptive. Yes, it was big, but his body was a straight line, whereas the bed was curved. Which meant he couldn't hug the outside edge and he really wasn't that far from her. He could hear her breathing; he could smell her, inhale her, as she and her delectable curves loomed there only about an inch away.

"Jake?" she whispered.

"Yeah."

He could hear her turn over and the sheets pulled taut her way. "Do you think," she began tentatively, reaching out a hand to touch his hair. He flinched. "Do you think maybe it would be easier on both of us if we just went ahead and did it and got it over with and, you know, got it out of our systems?"

"No." He set her hand back on her pillow.

"You sure?"

"Yes. Go to sleep, Zoë. Please." He rolled over so that he was facing the outer circle of vines. There was no way he was going to make things even worse by making love to her. Out of his system? Did she really think that would be the result? He barely knew her, and yet he already felt too entangled to leave. What would he feel if they shared something that intimate, if they wrapped themselves in each other for hours and hours and gave in to every little—and big—desire? He'd never be able to leave. And he'd never be able to live with himself or without her.

He reminded himself that the only reason he was here and the only reason he was staying was to find Toni. The only one. If he found her tomorrow, if he figured out what her scam was, he would be gone.

As much as he hated leaving Zoë in the lurch, once he figured out the mystery of Toni, he wouldn't have a choice—he would have to leave. Stay under false pretenses, pretending to be half of a honeymoon couple, just for the fun of it? He was an honorable guy. He had integrity. Morals. Ethics. Was he going to blow them all because he had the hots for a sweet, sexy woman who would never fit into his real life in a million years?

No, he couldn't do that. Not by a long shot.

If he really planned on leaving when his mission to find Toni was over, there had to be nothing between him and Zoë. Nothing. But in the meantime...

He wondered if it would work to lash himself to the

bed with jungle vines. Anything to keep him from going over to the other side of the bed.

Zoë's side.

HE WAS TOO TIRED to go to sleep. He knew she'd nodded off; her breathing was even and rhythmic over there. But all he did was stare up into those damn leaves and vines, wondering what he'd done to deserve this. Toss. Turn. Listen to her breathe. Remember feeling that same rhythm with his hand on her abdomen. Breathing together. In. Out. In. Out. Oh, lord. He was getting hard again. Swear. Toss. Turn some more. Wonder what she was dreaming about. Wish he could hold her. Doze off. Dream about making love to her. Wake up. Toss. Turn. Listen to her breathe...

Zoë had told him his karma was going to rise up and bite him in the butt. Looked like she was right.

And he had to find something else to think about. How about the search for Toni? That would be handy. How about creating some semblance of an investigation here?

He slipped out of the bed as quietly as he could, opening the drawer again, finding a pair of pants and a zipped jacket to throw over his shorts. The zipper made the slightest zzz as he pulled it up.

"Jake, what are you doing?"

He turned. Through the shadows, he could see Zoë sitting up in bed, holding back the vines, looking quite peeved.

"I didn't mean to wake you up," he told her. "Go back to sleep. It's only about three o'clock."

"What are you doing?"

He shrugged. "I couldn't sleep. I thought I'd..." He broke off. "I thought I'd go break into the Lodge and find where they're keeping our stuff. I want my notebook. I want to work on this Toni thing."

"Okay." She reached over to the bedside table and switched on the lamp. It, too, was decorated with leaves, and it cast a soft green glow into the bedroom. She hung her legs over the side and started to hunt around for her shoes.

"What are you doing?"

She looked up. "Going with you."

"Oh, no, you're not."

Already tying her shoes, she dismissed that notion with one wave of her hand. "Don't be stupid, Jake. I can either go with you or I can follow you and make a lot of noise and get us both into trouble and make you sorry you didn't bring me."

Damn her, anyway. Why did she have to keep pushing him? The whole idea was to be away from her. "Zoë, this isn't your mission."

"Sure it is. Besides, if we get caught and we're together, we can just, you know, rip off our clothes, throw our arms around each other and pretend we were into the whole doing-it-in-the-great-outdoors thing like everyone else around here," she said reasonably. "If you get caught alone, what excuse will you have?"

Good Lord, she was right. He certainly hoped they didn't have to rip off their clothes—he was under enough strain already—but it would be a perfect cover. "Sometimes you really scare me, you know that?"

She blinked. "Why?"

"You have a real criminal mind," he muttered, as she caught up with him and trailed him down the stairs.

"It's okay, Jake." She patted his arm. "If we're going to run around breaking and entering, one of us needs to be devious. And it's *so* not you."

As Zoë searched for the map of the grounds, Jake stopped in the kitchen and rifled the drawers. He ended up with a nutpick, a paring knife, one of the skewers intended for marshmallow roasting and a flashlight. Odd burglary tools, but they would have to do. He propped open the door for her, shining the light on the map as they took off down the path.

The main building, dubbed the Lodge on the map, was a lot closer than the Welcome Center had been, so it wasn't nearly as arduous a trip back as it had been earlier in the evening. It was eerie, though, traipsing through the darkness, and if there were any honeymooners braving the bushes to find a little loving in the wee hours, they were quiet about it.

Outside, with fresh air hitting his face, he felt a bit better. And he had to give credit to Zoë—she was quiet, she didn't giggle or complain or make a nuisance of herself, and it was really very useful to have a companion and a second pair of eyes. She didn't even seem scared. In fact, as he glanced over her way, he got the definite idea she was enjoying this. Given the sparkle in her eyes and the smile that kept playing around her lips, he concluded that Zoë got off on the concept of intrigue and skulduggery, even if they hadn't really run into any yet. He smiled, shaking his head. Somebody might as well enjoy it.

Spotlights flooded the main entrance to the Lodge, illuminating the sign and making their target clear. It was a large, sprawling building, constructed entirely of huge logs, with a wide, low roof and lots of windows. Except for the ever-present hum of crickets, all was quiet. Except for one corner of the Lodge, where windows were ablaze with light, all was dark. As Jake pulled up, wondering about the lights, he spotted golf carts parked outside those windows.

"They work late here," he murmured. He still thought

there was something fishy about this place. Why would spa personnel need to be working at three in the morning?

"Jake, I just realized." She took his arm, bending up to whisper in his ear. "There's twenty-four-hour room service, remember? They probably work out of here."

"You're right." She really was proving useful to have around. He probably wouldn't have remembered room service.

"So are we going to bag it?"

"Nope." He took her hand. "We're going to go in the back way. We're going to stay as far away as possible from that corner of the building. And be very quiet."

With Jake leading the way, they circled around to the side completely opposite all the lights, where he tried each of the windows in turn as Zoë played lookout. But the windows were all securely bolted from inside. Finally, around the back, they found a delivery entrance that looked a bit less formidable, and Zoë focused the beam of the flashlight on the door handle as Jake knelt and poked at it with the nutpick. All it took was a few jiggles and they were in.

Slowly, carefully, Jake opened the door, checking for lights or noise. So far, so good. Extinguishing the flashlight, he crept ahead, keeping her behind him, taking a path past a refrigerated storeroom, another housekeeping storeroom, and then a couple of offices, all closed up for the night. "It's awfully nice of them to stencil names on all the doors so we know what's inside," he remarked.

"What are we looking for?" she asked softly. "How will we know when we find it?"

"I don't know. Where would you store everybody's stuff for a week? A locker room? Maybe a safe?"

Zoë stopped, peering down a side corridor. "I've got Guest Services, Employee Locker Room and Guest Vault. That's what it says on the last door."

He considered. "Guest Vault sounds good to me." He knew the minute they opened the door and he ran his flashlight over a whole wall full of wire baskets that this was the right place. Each basket was neatly labeled, and each one had a small padlock. "Bingo."

"Uh-oh," Zoë whispered, looking at all the gleaming padlocks. "How do we get into those?"

"Not a problem." He was already skimming along, looking for his name. He found Zoë Kidd and Wylie Anderson, instead. "You'd think if they steal my wallet, with all my ID in it, they could at least get my name right on the damn basket."

"Shh," Zoë hissed. She was stationed with her ear to the door. "I think I hear someone coming."

Jake cut the light and crossed the room, pulling her behind the door with him so they'd be hidden if someone entered. Looping an arm around her for safekeeping, tugging her close, he could feel her heart racing against his. She tucked her head into his shoulder, holding her breath, and it made her seem vulnerable and small. He tightened his embrace. This was different from the unbridled lust he usually felt around Zoë. This was protective. This was…weird. His heart felt as if it had turned over in his chest.

Weird. They were breaking the law, and they could be in trouble if discovered. He had no badge, no ID and no weapon, and he should've been very concerned. But all he could think of was how right she felt in his arms and wonder how she would react if he tipped up her chin and kissed her.

Outside, voices and footsteps neared and Jake held

her even closer for a second, until whoever it was out there passed right by. "Phew," he sighed into her ear.

Reluctantly Jake swung back into action, setting her aside as if nothing had happened. Without a word, he returned to the Zoë and Wylie basket and got to work on disposing of the little padlock.

"Wow, you're good at the lock picking," she whispered.

"Thanks. It's a gift." Quickly he retrieved the duffel bag with his clothes in it, and then his badge, his wallet, his notebook, and his cell phone. Everything else in there was Zoë's. Gathering his belongings, he turned away from the basket. "Do you want anything?"

Zoë heaved a sigh. "Heavens, no. What are you taking all that junk for? I thought you just wanted your notebook."

"I want my stuff."

"Jake, someone is going to notice that our basket is now almost empty. And housekeeping is going to see all of that lying around the cottage." She lifted her hands in the air, palms up, as if in disbelief. "They'll know you stole it back."

"I don't care. If I'm going to break out of here, I want my own pants and my own shoes."

"Since when are you breaking out?" she inquired, planting her hands on her hips.

"Maybe. Maybe not. If I find Toni and get the goods on her, I can leave."

"You can't leave!" she contended. "The bus doesn't come back till Friday, remember? No in and out. And there's an electric fence. How can you possibly leave?"

"Keep it down, will you? We can argue about this later. Right now we need to get out of here before anyone else comes along." Shoving everything inside the duffel bag, he swept past Zoë, taking her arm and reaching for the door.

But she dug in her heels. "What kind of cop are you?" she said in a fierce undertone. "You're just going to leave, completely ignoring all those other baskets sitting there, full of other people's personal possessions that would tell you all about them? There's a whole lot of wallets and purses in those baskets."

Good point. It was against his nature to illegally search people's private possessions, but on the other hand he wasn't going to steal anything. He just needed a little info.

As he tried to think of a methodical way to conduct this search, he listened at the door for a long moment. "I don't think anyone else is coming back this way. But just to be on the safe side..." He clicked the lock on the door from the inside and moved a garbage can over in front of it.

And then he turned back to Zoë. "Okay, here's the deal. I'll go along and take off all the locks, then you go through and pull out women's driver's licenses, okay? I'll take another look-see for anything suspicious—I don't know what, but I'll just have to know it when I see it. You lay the licenses on the floor, and then we'll scan the pictures and the names, see if anybody jumps out. Then we put everything back and get the hell out of here."

"I'm glad you liked my idea," she said sweetly, moving into place, ready to begin sifting and sorting. "It's nice you have begun to appreciate my value as a team member."

Over his shoulder, he tossed, "Just don't say I told you so. I hate it when people say that."

"Aw, Jake, we gotta get you over these things. You hate a lot of things."

No comment.

It took a few minutes for him to go through the baskets, but he found absolutely nothing. By then, Zoë had made a neat grid of driver's licenses on the floor, but Jake surveyed the lot of them. "There are twenty couples, so there should be twenty women," he mused, stepping back. "But we only have eighteen driver's licenses."

"Well, there's me," Zoë said logically. "I didn't take mine out. So actually there should be nineteen."

"Who's the missing lady?"

"Oh, wait. Remember that one couple ditched at the airport," Zoë put in. "There are only nineteen couples here, not twenty."

"Okay, so twenty minus you and the one who ditched at the airport leaves us with eighteen. Who've you got with a name anything like Toni, first or last? And probably any other *T*'s, just to see."

"The name closest to Toni is Tonya," she noted, holding up that card. "Tonya Abbott, age twenty-five, five-six, a Scorpio, blond, blue eyes, from Hinsdale, Illinois."

"It says on there she's a Scorpio?" he said doubtfully.

"Of course not. But her birthday is here. Duh." She waved the driver's license. "I thought her Zodiac sign might be useful, you know, personalitywise. As a Scorpio, she's more likely to be secretive and deceptive."

Jake just stared at her. What the hell was she talking about?

"Okay, so then there's Tori," she went on, reaching for another ID. "We already know about her. She's twenty-eight, brunette, five-eight, and from Green Bay. She's a Capricorn. Couldn't you just tell? There is also a Joni whose last name is Antonini, a Tracey and a Tamyra, and a woman with the middle name Antonia." She squinted at the photo. "Mary Antonia Gerace, who happens to be the woman who sat across the aisle on the bus who was sure that we weren't newlyweds. Remember her?"

"It's not her," he said quickly. "She's too old."

"So toss Mary Antonia." She tucked that license back inside the purse in the right basket. "What age are we looking for?"

"I don't know." He tried to remember when his father had said she claimed to be born. Mid-seventies. Same age range as Sean, who was what, twenty-seven? "Under thirty, anyway."

"Okay. What with hair dye and Botox, it's hard to tell sometimes, but let's take out all the over-forties, which is only three, including Mary Gerace. That ought to be safe." Chewing her lip in concentration, she set about returning the licenses they didn't want. "Anything else that eliminates people?"

"She's white, medium height, slender build, a little bigger than you, maybe."

"Hmm...that safely eliminates two black women and one Asian, including Tamyra, two more who are, well, chubby, and Tracey, who is six-two." She stood up with a fistful of licenses. "That leaves us with nine contenders, including Tonya and Tori. Any other disqualifying factors?"

Right before his eyes, Zoë had turned into an FBI profiler. He was astonished. She was really very good at this. "She had longer hair than you, and it was blond when the photo was taken." He shrugged. "Aside from the foot evidence, that's all I've got."

"Did you say photo?"

"Yeah." She already knew so much he couldn't see the harm in admitting the rest. "My dad got a few lousy photos. The only good one is of the famous sparkly ho shoes."

"You have 'em on you? C'mon, turn 'em over, partner. Maybe that will help."

He pulled the blurry pictures out of the pocket at the back of his notebook, handing them to her one at a time. "I know they're terrible. If you knew Vince, the guy who took them, you would understand. He's..." But he stopped when he saw the look on her face. "What? Have you seen those shoes? Or someone who looks like her?"

"I don't know." Tilting her head to one side, shining the flashlight right on the photos, she stared at the foot picture. She had the strangest expression on her face. "No. I—I guess not."

"You sure?"

She nodded, but she still looked preoccupied.

Jake figured he could worry about that later. Right now, he was getting a little nervous about being in the Guest Vault for so long. "Well, let's look through the rest of the licenses and see if anyone fits the age and weight. And then let's get this stuff back in the baskets and get out of here already. At least we have some suspects, which is more than I had before. Then tomorrow we can try to get next to Tori and Tonya, see what they have to say for themselves."

Zoë sent him a speculative glance. "We?"

There was no use avoiding it. They were about as much of a "we" as was humanly possible at this point. Jake met her gaze. Guardedly he answered, "That's right. *We.*"

10

"ALL RIGHT, everyone," Tommy, their group leader, announced in a stage whisper. Since the room was dark, he held a flashlight up near his face. It cast his face into stark relief, making him look like a Boy Scout leader trying to scare the kids in his pack. "You've all done very well with the relaxation exercise, but it's time to move on to the confession session, which we'll be doing outside, in Explorer's Meadow." He crouched next to Jake, who had Zoë curled up, fast asleep in his lap. "How sweet. I guess you could say she's relaxed, all right."

Jake murmured, "I don't want to wake her up. We, uh, had a hard night."

Tommy's cheesy smile widened. "That's the whole idea behind the Explorer's Journey, Jake. We want you to explore all the boundaries of connubial bliss."

"Yeah. I saw the videos."

"Glad you enjoyed them."

"Didn't say that." Jake glanced down, smoothing away a tendril of red hair that curved over her cheek. Zoë had gone out like a light during the exercise, which was supposed to relieve tension. All he had to do was hold her in his lap, massage her temples with the tips of his fingers, and think of ten nice things to say about her. Not too tough. Not entirely comfortable for him, especially after she fell asleep curled up like a puppy next to the stove, but easy enough.

He hadn't expected her to drop off like that, but that was okay, even if he was trapped while she snoozed. But they were the only ones in the room at the moment who had ended up that way. They were also the only ones wearing all their clothes.

Quite a few of their journey compatriots were making out, right there in public, and the moans and groans were a little hard to ignore. Sure, the room was dark, with only a few candles around the outside edges, but what was it with these people? He'd never seen so many public displays of affection.

He stayed as far away from the others as possible. That made it hard to keep an eye on his top suspects Tonya and Tori, but there wasn't much to be seen, anyway. Scratch that. There was way too much to be seen.

Too bad he didn't know if Toni had any identifying marks like tattoos or scars. Because he sure could've seen those. If he'd wanted to gape at the lovemaking going on on all sides. Which he didn't.

He wasn't making much progress on any front at the moment. He told himself he was lulling Toni, wherever she was, into a false sense of security. Warming up. Getting ready to pounce.

Yeah, right.

"Time to wake up your wife and meet everyone else in the meadow," Tommy ordered. When Jake still didn't move to rouse Zoë, Mr. Clean added acerbically, "Have you noticed how often you two are bringing up the rear? Wouldn't you like to make up a little ground instead of slacking all the time?"

Bringing up the rear? Slacking? Oh, he'd noticed. Right before she fell asleep, Zoë was still apologizing about doing so poorly on the blindfolded balance-beam exercise, which, as per usual, Ron and Tori had dominated. All you had to do was guide your blindfolded partner down the beam. But although Jake did his best, Zoë fell off right away, unable to go where he told her. Jake just figured she was exhausted, although Tommy sneered that there was obviously trust lacking in their relationship.

Jake wanted to smash some trust down Tommy's throat.

Besides, Zoë had been distracted. She was much more concerned with chatting up suspect number three, Joni Antonini, about where she was from and what she did for a living rather than paying attention on the balance beam.

"I love your haircut," Zoë had opened with, cornering Joni. "Are you from Chicago? Did you get it cut there?"

Which led the unsuspecting Joni to say that no, she lived in Minneapolis. She'd gotten her hair cut there. It cost a lot but she had to have a good haircut because she was the weather girl on a TV station in Minneapolis and did Zoë think it was too blond? Before the conversation was over, Zoë pretty much knew Joni's whole life story. He was pretty sure Joni was too short and too wide in the hips to be Toni, anyway, but how cute that Zoë was willing to screw up the lesson to get info on a suspect and *he* was the one seriously trying to do it right. Yes, but he had so wanted to smoke Ron and Tori and knock some stuffing out of their smug confidence.

The next exercise had been some stupid painting thing. He and Zoë managed to do okay with face painting, and it was actually funny when he exacted payback for the blue face she gave him by drawing strawberries on her cheeks. She couldn't stop laughing, which made his strawberries look more like shapeless red blobs. But moving from faces to bodies was a lot trickier. They had both sort of backed off and insisted on sticking with faces and arms, which started a whole brouhaha with the staff member who was running the painting exercise.

Zoë's face flushed as red as the strawberry paint when she said she did not want her breasts painted and she refused to do Jake's chest, either. "I don't want to do this in front of other people. And seeing too much of my fellow campers is turning me *off!*" she'd snapped, which made Jake laugh.

"You're not communicating very well on a sensual level," the man in charge said sadly. "You need to trust your partner, and tap into your desire. *Own* your desire. *Embrace* your desire. Become *one* with your desire."

"We're fine," Zoë argued. "We don't need to be throwing paint on each other to communicate on a sensual level or any other level. We have a whole lot of levels to choose from, Jake and I, which I cannot say for my fellow campers, who all seem to communicate on one level only. Which would be sex."

"You need to get past that shame-and-blame behavior," the guy responded with a whole lot of condescension. "You need to concentrate on yourselves and keep your nose out of other people's business."

Ouch. Jake knew she wasn't going to take that well. Figuring discretion was the better part of valor, he stepped back to enjoy the show, although he felt sorry for the poor clueless employee.

"Not my business?" she demanded, brandishing her paintbrush like a sword. "It becomes my business when they keep rubbing my nose in their business."

"Your hang-ups are not part of the Explorer's Journey," the man responded coldly. "Get over it."

Which really made her mad. "I *own* my hang-ups,"

she said angrily, stabbing at him with her paintbrush. "I *embrace* my hang-ups. I am *one* with my hang-ups. And I am not giving them up for you or anyone else!"

Which, in the end, meant another lecture from Tommy. Jake felt as if he was in kindergarten, and he was going to be denied recess privileges any minute now.

But it amused him to know that Zoë had made up hang-ups on the spot just to protect him. They both knew she didn't care about the naked green and purple breasts and bottoms around them. Hell, she probably would've been happy to just ignore it or laugh it off if she had been there with a more accommodating partner. But she thought it made Jake uncomfortable, so she was pretending for his sake.

Well, that was something. He now had a handle on how Zoë's mind worked.

Chanting "Together Forever, No Matter What," practicing couples meditation until he hyperventilated, holding her hand to guide her on the balance beam, painting strawberries on Zoë's cheeks. And that was all before lunch. The stuff they made them do kept getting crazier and crazier. But what was the craziest part? That he was starting to enjoy it? Or that he was starting to understand her?

Jake wondered if his team had made up any bonus points for relaxation, given that he'd just had about ten major epiphanies and Zoë was still peacefully dozing in his lap.

"Wake her up," Tommy commanded. "Let's get outside. Now. We're behind schedule."

Sounded like Tommy boy needed to take a few of his own serenity lessons. "Go ahead without us. I don't want to wake her up," Jake returned.

"I am starting to wonder why you two even came on this journey," Tommy said, narrowing his eyes. They were pretty small to begin with, so that made them almost disappear. "If you're going to continue to underachieve this way, we may have to do some one-on-one sessions to examine your motives for being here."

Ah, threatening harsh bright lights and rubber hoses, huh? And Jake had thought it would be so easy to blend in.

Still, as he gazed down at Zoë, so peaceful, sleeping so sweetly, he really didn't want to make her get up. She deserved a nap. After all, it was his fault they'd gone burglarizing in the middle of the night, and then when they got back to the cabin, they'd stayed up plotting strategy and theorizing about suspects. It had been fun. Way more fun than lying in that stupid leafy bed obsessing over every sigh, every whisper of sound from Zoë's side.

"Way more fun," he said out loud. But Tommy was glaring at him, and he finally shook Zoë gently. "Wake up, sunshine. Time to go to confession session, whatever that means."

"Conjunction junction?" she asked drowsily. "Like *Sesame Street*?"

"Something like that."

Still half asleep, she shook her head. But she stumbled behind him, out of the building and into the open air, into a cleared space rounded by flowers. It was a beautiful summer afternoon, a little less humid under a bright and shining sun. Most everyone was clothed, which was a big plus.

"Face each other in meditation pose," Tommy instructed. "Hurry up. Everyone else is already here."

So Jake led Zoë to the last pair of grass mats, where

they dutifully sat opposite each other, cross-legged, hands up, palm-to-palm.

"Very good," Tommy said unctuously.

Zoë was yawning and sleepy, so she had an excuse for being a bit out of it, but that didn't cover the rest of the crowd. When Jake ventured a look around, he once again had the impression that there was something cult like going on here. They all looked stoned. Or maybe as if they'd been mainlining Spanish fly and oysters. All heavy lids and salacious smiles, they stared captivated into each other's eyes, and you could practically see the heady vapors of lust and desire floating in the air.

They hadn't all been crazed sex fiends on the bus. Were Tommy and his helpers putting something in their food? Was it in the air? Maybe an outgrowth of all the exercises? Or just normal honeymoon behavior that seemed strange to Jake because he'd never had a honeymoon?

"Zoë, are you awake yet?" he whispered across their clasped hands.

"Uh-huh."

"Look around. Do people seem weird to you?"

She was supposed to be maintaining eye contact with him, but she quickly did a scan of the couples on their grass mats in the meadow. "Well, they all look horny. Is that it?"

"I'll tell you later," he muttered as Tommy came strolling by.

"Good, good, everyone. I will ask you a question, and first, each wife should answer it, being as completely honest as possible. That's why we call it the confession session." He beamed at them. "Once your wife has answered, husbands, please validate what she has told you by repeating it back to her. No other comments. Just echo what she tells you. Everybody got it?"

Dopey, lust-filled nods all around.

"Good, good," Tommy announced, in the oiliest possible tone. "First question. Wives, tell your husbands about your greatest failure. All right? Do we have that?" Placing his hands together in a prayerful attitude, he oozed, "What do you feel is your greatest failure?"

Zoë's eyes were wide-open now, and he knew she didn't want to tell him. Hell, he wouldn't have wanted to share his failures with her, either. Damn this stupid place, for pushing them both. He wouldn't have cared if they were married. He still thought people ought to have a right to some pride and some dignity and not go throwing their failures around. Not that she had to answer honestly. She could say she struck out in Little League when she was ten or something. Not that she would. Not Zoë.

Meanwhile, what the hell was he going to say when it was his turn? So far, the search for Toni was shaping up as his biggest failure. And he had no intention of sharing that info.

Around them, while others mumbled their confessions. Zoë remained silent.

"Zoë?" Tommy leaned down. "Are you thinking of something?"

"Maybe you should pick falling off the balance beam," Jake said helpfully. "Or me screwing up the test the first day."

"That's hardly her failure. And you shouldn't be prompting her," Old Baldy interrupted with a scowl. "She needs to air her failings to get past them. She needs to get in touch with her own feelings of inadequacy and trust you to understand her feelings. You two are at a real crossroads here. Do you want to begin to explore the reasons you seem unable to trust each other? Or try to work toward growing and evolving?"

Grudgingly Jake accepted that. After all, Zoë was the one who wanted to be part of this program. Presumably for moments just like this, no matter how painful he found them. He already knew what her answer had to be, anyway. Wylie.

Wylie, he mouthed.

"Wylie?" she echoed.

Jake nodded. "It's okay, Zoë, bring it on. You can do it."

"No comments till she's done," Tommy interjected sternly, leaning in with his hand on Jake's shoulder.

So Jake just kept nodding, looking her right in the eye, and finally Tommy toddled off to torment someone else.

"Go ahead," Jake whispered, as soon as the jerk was gone. In some strange way, he wanted to hear this, wanted to know exactly what the deal was with the man she was supposed to marry. "Tell me about Wylie."

"Well, okay, but I don't know what to say," she admitted. "Definitely a failure. I mean, the honeymoon was paid for. I had a dress and a place and a cake. I thought I wanted to get married, but I guess I didn't." Her expression was glum. "Not really. I mean, when push came to shove, I couldn't."

She was still keeping her gaze on his, as instructed, but she looked all crumpled and upset, and he hated putting her through this. Still, a part of him was curious. He found himself wanting to know who the guy was and what had happened between them. Hardly moving his lips so no one would hear him talking when he wasn't supposed to be, Jake murmured, "Did you love him? What happened?"

She bit her lip. Her poor lip. He wanted to be able to talk to her, to tell her not to chew on her lip, to ask her questions and reassure her. Jake, the silent man, was having a heck of a time keeping his mouth shut.

"You know, you're right, Jake. I was thinking of something else, but the thing with Wylie really is a big failure on my part, isn't it?" Zoë clasped her fingers through his instead of keeping them flat, which was against the rules, but Jake was hardly going to rat on her. "I've never told anyone this, but he cheated on me. More than once, I think. Which, I know, does not sound like my failure. I mean, let's face it, is it really my fault if Wylie was a dog?"

"Hell, no." Of course it wasn't her fault!

"Still, I consider it my failure because, because I keep having these feelings that maybe I sabotaged it from the start," she said darkly. She gripped his hands more tightly. "Wylie wasn't like you, Jake. He wasn't strong or dependable or sure, you know? You always seem so sure."

Little did she know.

"Maybe I didn't give enough or maybe I wasn't supportive enough and he just couldn't hack it, you know? He told me he wouldn't have cheated if I'd just trusted him, but that is so backward. How could I trust him if he was going to cheat? I mean, my not trusting him was right on the money."

Her eyes filled with tears. Angry tears, not mopey tears, but Jake didn't want to see her cry. Ever. He was starting to hate Wylie, wherever and whoever he was. He also hated Tommy for making them do this exercise. He knew hate was not part of the Explorer's Journey, and yet hate was what he was feeling.

"I think I am a terrible person." She was rushing her

words now, clutching his hands so fiercely he was afraid he was going to lose all the feeling in his fingers. "I lied to myself and I lied to him, and I promised I would never, ever do that again, and then you walk in my door, and here I am, doing it again!"

He kept his voice very low. "Because we lied about being a couple, you mean? I don't exactly get that part."

But she wasn't paying attention. She was way too far gone on confession mode, wound up about Wylie and letting loose. "I think poor Wylie had to screw up on purpose to push me, you know, to the end of my rope," she declared. "Because then I would kick him out and he didn't have to leave, because he was too much of a chicken to end it himself! He was a chicken and I didn't love him or trust him enough, and at some point, I am just going to have to admit to myself that I am a rotten person and a terrible girlfriend and it's no wonder it didn't work. I screw up everything!"

And then she did start to cry, full out, and Jake absolutely couldn't stand it. He reeled her in by her hands, pulling her up against him, holding her tight. "It's okay, Zoë. It wasn't your fault. Any guy who would cheat on you has to be out of his mind. He was a faithless pig, and don't worry about it, okay?" He stroked her hair. "As soon as we get back to Chicago, you show me where he is and I will personally beat the crap out of him for cheating on you. That's a promise."

"You two have fallen out of the pose. And you don't appear to be echoing, Jake," Tommy noted smartly. "Was that echoing I heard? I don't think so, Jake."

"My wife isn't feeling well," Jake shot back. He stood up, bringing Zoë with him. "I think it may be the food here. Something is making her sick."

Tommy stepped back, flustered. "Oh, I'm sure it's not

the food. The confession sessions can be very stressful, it's true. But also cathartic. I'm sure she'll be fine—"

"Nope. I'm going to take her back to our cabin so she can lie down. When she feels better—*if* she feels better— we'll come back for more exercises." Jake swept her up into his arms. She looked about as shocked as Tommy, but Jake didn't care. He tightened his hold and strode across the field, making for the path up the hill, back to their cottage.

"Jake," she put in, sliding one hand along his cheek and trying to turn his face. Her words bounced up and down with his strides. "I'm fine. You don't need to carry me. And you don't need to beat up Wylie. While I appreciate the offer, really, no! No beating anyone up on my behalf. I'm fine."

The path was beginning to angle up sharply, so Jake was happy to put her down. He was in good shape, but not good enough to carry a woman, even a small one, all the way up a steep hill. As he set her down, he explained, "Listen, I just couldn't take that stupid confession garbage anymore. You started to cry, Zo."

"You just called me Zo. Like you have a pet name for me." She smiled, bracketing his face with her hands. "Sometimes, Jake, you are just too cute to be believed. And carrying me out of there...and offering to smack down Wylie. What am I going to do with you? Could you be any cooler? Could you be any more of, like, a *gift?*"

"Thanks. I think."

"My karma. Your karma. The two of hearts. What a great thing! Am I lucky or what?" None of which made any sense to him, but she seemed thrilled.

Out of nowhere, Zoë reached up and kissed him, tangling one hand around the back of his neck. It was quick and hot, sweet and adorable. Nothing like the first time, which was all passion and power. This one, where she was in charge, was about spontaneity and joy. Too bad it also tasted like *more*. It didn't take much these days to get him up and moving, raring for action, and that kiss was enough. When she stepped back, laughing, breathless, he automatically tried to drag her back into his arms.

But she was practically dancing up the path. "Don't think I didn't notice you staged your rescue in perfect time so you didn't have to confess your biggest failure."

"Me?" He tried to recover his ability to think instead of just reacting. "Who said I ever failed at anything?"

"Well, there was that empathy test."

"That wasn't my fault," he protested.

"Jake, Jake. *Own* your failures. *Embrace* your failures. Become *one* with your failures," she teased, doing a fair impression of that blowhard Tommy.

He nodded wisely. "So even you are admitting that the program is ridiculous and these people are all nuts."

"Not exactly." Zoë stopped in the middle of the path. "Okay, at least kind of ridiculous. Sometimes. But there's good stuff here, underneath. Look how much better you know me than when we started. And it's only been one day! Well, two. Three if you count the night we met."

God. It felt like about three years. He was certain he'd aged about ten years.

"And look how happy everyone seems. Happy doesn't exactly capture it, does it?"

"More like stoned out of their minds."

"Like, on drugs? You really think so?"

He pondered it for a minute. "There's sure something going on."

"Uh-oh," she said.

"What?"

"I just realized we are footloose and fancy-free now that we've ditched confession session." She grabbed him by the jacket, patting down his pockets, jumping up close, and he had the immediate urge to haul her up even closer and kiss her senseless.

They weren't that far from the lovers' swing. Maybe a few lunges and plunges back and forth would be just what the doctor ordered. Jake considered the wisdom in that plan. Not very wise. But it might be a heck of a lot of fun.

But Zoë demanded, "Do you still have your burglary tools on you?" and his mind shifted off the lovers' swing.

"No, why?"

"We know everyone else is busy confessing. What better time to do a little looking around?" Her eyes began to sparkle with enthusiasm. "Like in Tori and Ron's cabin. I know they're in Number five down by the lake because I chatted them up and asked. And Tonya and her husband are in Number fourteen, not far from us."

"Zoë, you scare me, but you have great ideas," he concluded, already catching her hand and making a beeline for their cottage to pick up his handy nutpick. Under his breath, he added, "How did I ever get along without you?"

He couldn't believe he'd said that. Although Zoë shot him a funny look, she was wise enough not to offer a response.

She didn't need to. He had already said it to himself. *Jake, my boy, you are in a powerful amount of trouble.*

THEY KNOCKED OVER Tonya's cabin first, and found absolutely nothing. Tori and Ron's place was neat as a pin, with equally unimpressive results. Well, they now knew that Tori and Ron had been watching videos of randy doctors and naughty nurses, but other than that, nothing.

Zoë was starting to feel as if it had not been the world's brightest idea to go ransacking other people's cottages in the middle of the afternoon, both because Jake kept looking all droopy eyed and jumpy, clearly exhausted, and also because she realized that no one had anything really useful or provocative in their cabins because the Explorer's Journey had told them not to bring it. No computers with suspicious files. No Palm Pilots with addresses and phone numbers. No datebooks or address books or photos of themselves that matched Jake's blurry pictures.

Not that it mattered. She looked over at Jake, who happened to be locking the door on Tori and Ron's cabin, ready to get out of there. "So, tell me, Zoë, now that you've had a chance to look at all the other women here *after* you saw the photo, what do you think? We eliminated Joni, right?"

"Uh-huh."

"How about Tonya and Tori? Or anyone else?"

"No," she said vaguely. "Not really."

Not really. *Zoë, Zoë, your pants are bursting into flame even as we speak,* she told herself. She chewed on a nail.

She wished he hadn't brought up the photo. She wished she'd never seen the photo.

Caught up in her enthusiasm for the puzzle and for hanging out with Jake, feeling like James Bond, Sherlock Holmes, Miss Marple and all three Charlie's Angels all rolled into one, she had momentarily forgotten the damn photo. And she had forgotten the fact that she knew something Jake didn't.

"Toni" wasn't anywhere near the Explorer's Journey. She never had been. The minute Jake showed Zoë the picture, the minute she held it in her hand, her mind had flashed back to the woman who never got on the bus, the one who'd had a fight with her husband and walked away before the bus ever left Chicago.

It wasn't the sparkly shoes or the blurry pictures that clued her in. It was just a feeling. But a very strong one. The more she looked at the other women around her, the more she knew she was right. Not one of the eighteen women in camp matched that photo. None of them matched the energy or the aura or whatever you wanted to call it. But the one woman who didn't get on the bus, the woman who was yelling and flailing her arms at her tattooed husband—*she* did. Zoë was certain.

Zoë knew she should tell him. But it was so mixed up!

She'd had the perfect opportunity in confession session. What was her biggest failure? How about failing to tell Jake she knew his mission was doomed? How about failing to trust him enough to tell him the truth?

But she already knew he would ask where she came up with her Toni info and she would say she just knew, she had mysterious psychic powers rising up and knocking her in the head all of a sudden, and he would laugh in her face.

And if, by some weird kismet, he believed her, then things would be even worse. Because he would be out of that camp and over the wall so fast the electric fence wouldn't have a chance to zing him on the way out.

Guilt. Guilt. Guilt.

Was it so wrong to keep him in the dark and keep him around? They were having such fun. She wanted him here. He liked being here. He was supposed to be her true love, but she wouldn't have a chance to convince him of that if he took off after some hussy in sparkly plastic shoes!

"We took too long," he grumbled. "I can hear people coming back from the meadow. And we have no reason to be down by the lake cabins, either."

"It's okay. Remember Plan B." She'd been hoping they'd get to use Plan B, the one where they leaped off the path or onto a picnic bench and pretended to be making love.

"Nope. No one coming."

Darn it, anyway. She'd been so hoping for a little pretend nookie, just a little. Because if they started it, maybe they could turn it into something more real.

That about summed up the whole experience so far, didn't it? Start by pretending but hope for something real.

Jake was farther ahead on the path now, but he turned back. "Are you coming?"

"Yeah, yeah. Right behind you."

Consumed with guilt, eaten up by lust and longing, Zoë chased after Jake. Chasing Jake had become a way of life these past few days. But it wasn't easy.

What was she going to do with him? And, what was she going to do about herself?

11

ZOË HAD NO INTENTION of letting Jake go through another sleepless night. As they both puttered around, sort of warily eyeing the bed, she offered, "Listen, I have some antihistamines in my makeup bag. I brought them with me."

"Why?"

Why? What difference did it make? Sometimes Jake could be so aggravating. "I've never been camping and I wasn't sure what things would be like here," she explained as patiently as she could manage. "I didn't want to be allergic and sneezing the whole time."

"Allergic to what?"

"I don't know. That's not the point." She held out a couple of bright yellow pills. "Here. Take these."

He just sort of looked at her balefully with those beautiful blue eyes, clearly not getting the point. "I don't have allergies."

"That's not the point!" she said again, louder this time. She worked on serenity every day, and every night, alone with Jake, she lost every bit of what she'd learned.

Zoë rebraided her hair, really tight, and fastened it on top of her head. What was she going to do with him?

The two of them had reached a sort of truce, where by day, they interrogated other people as often as possible, compiled as much info as possible, tried to do the exercises and lessons as well as possible—which had still not worked all that well. By night, they tried to stay out of each other's way as much as possible—which had not worked all that well, either—lust and longing were still the order of the day, and every time they turned around, they were reminded why everyone had come on the Explorer's Journey. Great sex. Which they all appeared to be getting. Frequently.

Except for Zoë and Jake. Which was why it was so easy to snap at him and get irritated with him. Because everyone else was sated and satisfied, and she was going bananas!

Mmm...bananas.

The yummy EJ products that smelled like bananas and coconut were weirdly mixed up in her mind with wanting Jake. It didn't make much sense, but she felt like Pavlov's dog—the minute she smelled the stuff, she thought of Jake rubbing the scented soap against his bare skin and she started to salivate.

"Okay, so my lack of allergies is not the point," he said tersely, bringing her back to reality and away from the mental image of his bare, soaped-up skin. "What is?"

"Antihistamines can make you drowsy. I know you couldn't sleep again last night, so I thought if you took some antihistamines tonight, you could drop right off."

"Nah." He moved toward the bathroom. "You go ahead. I'll just take a shower."

"You've been taking six showers a day."

"I like to be clean." He gave her a rueful smile. "It's okay. I think I'll sleep tonight. I feel better since I changed the soap."

Zoë lifted her eyebrows. How odd. She'd just been

thinking about soap. "What do you mean, you changed the soap?"

"The smell of that fruit-salad soap was starting to make me feel a little, um, sick," he mumbled. "So I stole a bar of plain old soap out of the employee locker room at the Lodge. Plus I've been trying not to breathe through my nose. Much better."

"Oh." It was a little disappointing. She really, really liked the pineapple-coconut smell. She had great fantasies when she went to sleep after using the lotions, which was helpful, since Jake was being so good about keeping his hands off, so fantasies were all she had. But if it made him ill... "Do you want me to not use the lotion or the bath gel or the shampoo? I can do that."

"No, no. If you like it..."

But then he gazed at her, and there were licks of flame in his gorgeous eyes. His nostrils flared slightly, and she could see he was definitely breathing through his nose. She could also see the tortured look in his eyes as he inhaled.

Oh, my God. He is so turned-on and trying so hard not to be. She felt the impact of that discovery deep in the pit of her stomach. At this point, she would've thought that after tossing and turning every night, Jake was too exhausted to have any libido left. But the haunted look on his face, the way he closed his eyes and stood very still for a moment, collecting the shreds of his self-control... If this situation was difficult for her, it was obviously driving Jake nuts. Jake, so strong, so controlled, was on the verge of losing it. Yikes.

His voice was rough and shaky when he asked, "About the soap and the gel...would you mind?"

"Of course not," she said slowly. If it would make Jake feel better, she would do it in a heartbeat. But there was something else going on here. Something she hadn't quite put her finger on. "Jake?"

He turned back from the bathroom door. "What?"

"Nothing." She scooted over there and held out the yellow pill. "Take the antihistamine, Jake. You look like hell. You need the sleep."

He took the tablet. "You swear this is just an antihistamine? You wouldn't give me anything weird, would you?"

"Of course not." She ought to be insulted, but she was too worried.

And then he closed the door, and she heard water running, so she knew he was safely back in the shower. Blowing out a long puff of air, she sat on the edge of the bed. Her head was too full of erotic images to think clearly, and it had been that way since...day one. Since she started using the EJ products, and pineapple-coconut-banana fumes invaded her consciousness.

She had just assumed it was being near Jake all the time. He was a very hot man, and he was always in the shower, so she had these mental pictures of soaking wet, naked Jake or lathered, naked Jake, soaping up and rinsing down. Right now, just conjuring up that image for a second, she was already aroused and shaking with desire. Whether he was in the shower or not, the thoughts were still there. If she was in his lap for some stupid exercise, all she could think about was what exactly was underneath her; if he was holding her hand or they were huddled together, hiding behind a tree, or she brushed up against him even the slightest, all she could think about was *sex, sex, sex*.

Zoë stood up and paced back and forth. She had assumed all those feelings were perfectly natural, and maybe they were. "I was attracted to him before we got here, and he was attracted to me, too," she argued with herself. Yes, but not like *this*.

Plus Jake kept insisting that everyone looked drugged, or the cooks were putting something in the food, or the mosquito-abatement fog had aphrodisiacs in it. Why hadn't he thought of the omnipresent EJ products, which the camp personnel pushed at every turn?

Zoë raised her hands to press her temples, trying to calm herself, but she caught a whiff of the leftover, lingering traces of coconut and banana in the oil she'd used for sensory massage class. Sniff.

And suddenly the idea that Jake was so near, so handy, was sharp and clear and bright in her mind. Jumbled words like "must have Jake" and "want Jake" and "jump in the shower with Jake" and "must get hands and mouth on Jake *now*" did a Tilt-a-Whirl inside her brain.

Yanking her hands away, she wiped them on a towel, and then raced down the stairs to the other bathroom, where she turned on the hot water and rinsed her hands again and again, like an X-rated version of Lady Macbeth. And then she opened the front door and the sliding door, trying to get a cross-breeze to air out the place. She stood on the deck next to the hot tub, gulping fresh, piney air, hoping for some mental clarity. How had she not noticed before?

"It's as plain as the nose on my face," she whispered. Of course, the fact that they were all addled with lust helped keep the secret. No one was thinking clearly.

But now it all added up. So many people were running to the store at the Lodge every day between sessions, stocking up on creams and gels and powders and soaps to take home with them, and she'd heard more than one employee reassuring desperate campers that they could order more after they left if they ran out. "See, we're packing up orders now," one of them had said, waving an arm at a stack of brown boxes labeled *Explorer's Journey*. "People can't get enough of our products. We send a truck out every day."

Desperate campers. Like addicts.

Of course, she hadn't said anything to Jake about it because she didn't want him to know about the trucks, because she had this feeling he would hop one and be out of her life in five seconds flat, especially since—of course—he had pretty much eliminated all the suspects who could be Toni. Zoë also knew why nobody fit the Toni profile—because none of them were Toni—but she kept her mouth shut on that one, too.

Deception, deception, deception.

Poor Jake. Even though *he* had stopped using the EJ gunk, even though he'd figured out he was better off if he stopped breathing through his nose—which was so adorable and yet the goofiest thing she'd ever heard—he was still getting vestiges of it off the skin and hair of everyone around him, including Zoë. If the pictures in his brain were anything like the pictures in her brain, he must be hanging on by his fingernails to his last shred of self-control.

"Why would they do this?" she asked out loud, trying to convince herself it had to be a joke. "What can it possibly gain them to send coconut-addicted sex zombies back to the real world?"

Well, that was obvious. Once hooked on the stuff, would they really want to stop using it? And where would they get it? How about the Explorer's Journey, the sole supplier?

Zoë could just imagine some poor, sobbing newlywed, back from the trip to Wisconsin, bored and listless, no longer able to have hot sex in the lover's swing, dialing in to plead with Tommy to please send a case of bubble bath—now! She already craved more of the stuff, and she'd only washed it off about thirty seconds ago.

Zoë shot back up the stairs, opened the window over the dresser, and flapped her arms to try to air things out. She stuck her head out the window and took a few more deep breaths, just to be sure she was operating under pure, unadulterated oxygen.

The door to the bathroom opened. Jake stepped out, wearing nothing but the official EJ drawstring pants, and her eyes swept up and down his chest. She loved the way his hard muscles sloped and curved, the way that little tracing of hair etched a path between his ribs down to his flat, delicious stomach, disappearing under the drawstring. Her mouth watered. It would take so little to pull the string, open that package, and have what she wanted and needed so desperately.

And why not? Why not go for it?

Maybe because he doesn't love you? Maybe because you are both operating under the influence of unknown pharmaceuticals?

"I don't care!" she said out loud.

He narrowed his eyes. "About what?"

"Nothing!" Damn whoever thought up the Explorer's Journey, she thought fiercely, for sticking Viagra up their noses and making all the clothes so easy to get out of. She wanted him, and the wanting was getting stronger every second. She waved her arms wildly, hoping to get rid of any last trace of the aphrodisiac scent.

"What are you doing?" he asked.

"Just trying to get rid of the coconut smell."

"Okay," he said doubtfully. He moved toward the dresser and pulled out a clean shirt.

"Jake?"

He turned, his face expectant. "What?"

But she looked at that face and she just couldn't wrap her mouth around the truth. *You were right—they're drugging people, and it's in the fruit-salad soap. Yes, I know you need to run off and report this and bring down the arm of the law on bad, bad Camp Feelgood, but could you wait and make love to me for about ten hours first? Oh, and after you do that, could you decide I'm the love of your life, too?*

"Jake, I..." Nope. Couldn't do it. Later, she told herself. Later she would tell him about the aphrodisiacs in the soap and the trucks and even about Toni. She would tell him. She would. Later. Like, maybe in the morning. "Did you take the antihistamine? Are you feeling drowsy?"

"Yeah, I am." He even yawned.

"Good, good. Ready to go to bed, then? I know I am." She faked a yawn of her own. Gingerly she edged around to her side and slid between the sheets, as Jake doused the lights and climbed in, too.

Silence. Was he asleep?

Guilt sat on her chest like a three-hundred-pound gorilla. She had always thought of herself as an honest person, and yet here she was, keeping big, ugly secrets. *Yes, but he's the cop, not me,* she argued with herself. *Why should I be responsible for clueing him in when he could've figured it out as easily as I did? Who died and made me the chief detective?* In fact, he was probably going to be even madder that she saw the handwriting on the wall and he had missed it. He was very competitive.

On the other hand, he was also a guy. He probably had so much testosterone surging through his veins at this point that he would never see straight again. For all she knew, he was going to explode with frustration and desire. That couldn't be good for him. Maybe it would be a good idea to get them both into a better mood before they confronted their confessions.

She shifted, rustling the bed linens as she turned in his direction. "Jake?" she whispered into the darkness.

"Yeah." He sounded a little testy but otherwise okay.

How to put this? "I was thinking maybe we could..." No that wasn't right. "I was thinking, for purely therapeutic reasons, since we're both kind of edgy, maybe we should—"

"Stop right there," he interrupted, his words slashing over hers. He'd gone from mildly annoyed to totally cranky. "If you're going to tell me again that we should make love just to get it over with—don't. Whatever you do, don't say that. Just to get it over with or for any other reason. Don't say it, Zoë."

"Well, I..."

He muttered something indistinguishable, but it sounded like, "Don't push me. It won't take much."

"What?"

"Nothing. Just don't say it. Please."

"That's not what I was going to say," she said defensively.

Of course, that was exactly what she was going to say. She'd been eating, sleeping and dreaming about making love with him, and she felt certain he was in the same, desire-infused boat. She had to tell him about what was going on, didn't she? And couldn't she clear her mind—and make them both feel a lot more able to cope—by getting the big nasty out of the way first?

Why not? He was fabulous, with his hard abs and his muscled chest and his narrow hips and his wonderful, wonderful butt, which was one of the all-time great butts! And he was right there, in her bed.

"Why is it such a terrible idea?" she whispered, coming a bit more unhinged with every breath she took. Her cards had come right out and told her he was her true love, and completely aside from the stupid coco-banana mind meld, she was surer with every passing moment that it was true. "Jake," she said more distinctly, "I think we should..."

Make love. *Because I am in love with you and you are under the power of some strange sex drug, and while it lasts, I'd like to get my licks in.*

No. Not what she wanted to say.

"I think it might be good for us to..."

Make love. *Because at least it would be love on my side, no matter what it is on your side, so just give me what I want and stop protesting, okay?*

Even worse.

"Jake?"

"Zoë, spit it out," he commanded. "I am really, really tired. So could you please say it and get it over with?"

Zoë let out an "arrggh" sound and stuffed her head into her pillow. How flattering was it to have to beg a man, even one hopped up on some strange sex drug, to make love to you?

Not. And Zoë Kidd pushed herself sexually on no man. In Jake's eyes, she might be a total flake, but she was not a slutty flake. A girl had to have some pride!

"Zoë?" He lifted his head. "What did you want to say?"

"Just that..." She sank back into the bedsheets, giving up. "I wanted to say thank you for everything you've done. You've been very sweet and kind and generous and—"

"Okay, okay, enough already."

"No, but I mean it." And that, at least, was true. "It's

been wonderful, Jake, being here with you. You are wonderful. Gallant, you know, carrying me off like a white knight because you didn't want to see me cry, trying so hard to do these exercises when I know you think they're completely idiotic. No one has ever tried so hard for me."

She paused. She was making herself feel even guiltier for not coming clean with him, given that she really did mean every word she was saying.

Slowly, carefully, she told him, "Whatever else happens, Jake, I just wanted you to know that I really am glad to have gotten to know you and I hope all of this hasn't been too painful for you. I feel really lucky that you came along on this trip with me."

Jake didn't say anything. But he reached over and took her hand inside his, lifting it to his lips. And then his gentle, clever lips brushed her fingers, and Zoë melted from the inside out.

Did he know what he did to her? Did he know he was not what she thought was her type, not the right match at all, and yet he was everything she'd ever wanted?

At that moment, with his mouth on her hand, she would have bet her life on the fact that these feelings had absolutely nothing to do with any soap or lotion voodoo. This was *them*. This was real.

His breath puffed against her fingers when he said, "I got lucky, too. Who knew that I would go off on a wild-goose chase for a con woman and run into someone like you?"

Toni. Right in the midst of all her bliss, Zoë was struck with guilt all over again. Now would be the perfect time, when they were all warm and friendly and comfy, to tell him the truth, to bring up the psychic thing and why she started this trip and how she knew about Toni. But she just couldn't. She just couldn't ruin everything.

She slipped her hand away and brought it back to her own side of the bed.

She remembered identifying her greatest fear on that empathy exam the first day. Her heart slipped a beat just thinking about it. *My greatest fear would be watching the love of my life walk away.*

And what exactly would Jake do if she told him there was no Toni, and she'd known it for days? He wouldn't stick around, that was for sure.

Every day, they did lessons on communication, and the two of them did fine. Every day, they did lessons on serenity, and they managed to bungle their way through. Every day, they learned about harmony and anger management and empathy, and they did okay. But every day, when it came to the trust exercises, Zoë knew she was holding back. Did she trust him to guide her along the balance beam? No. Did she trust him to paint her intimate areas? No. Did she trust him with her deepest secrets?

No. She told him about Wylie, but that was easy because Wylie was no longer important to her. She'd hedged her bets and avoided the real stuff, the stuff about how she didn't want to trust Jake because she was afraid he would walk away. Fear. Lack of trust. Heart-break.

She tried to remember to breathe. It sounded as if he had fallen asleep over there, and she hoped he had. He needed the rest. And maybe if he was sleeping she wouldn't be so tempted to roll over to his side.

She hitched up on her elbow and edged over close enough that she could see him in the dark. Sleeping or awake, he was one beautiful man. He took her breath away.

"Jake, if you aren't my true love, I don't think one exists," she whispered. "But how do I trust you enough to tell you that? How do I make you love me, too?"

On the wall of the bedroom, the Explorer's Journey motto, entwined in painted leaves and wines, seemed to mock her.

Together Forever, No Matter What.

Yeah, right. Not for her and Jake, who barely had a chance at tomorrow, let alone forever.

JAKE WAS CERTAINLY feeling peppy today. A little sleep would do that, he thought. He wished he'd known about antihistamines ages ago.

He rubbed his hands together with glee. Today, whatever the goons had in store for them, he planned to kick some booty. It was great. He could concentrate on winning at the lesson, keep his mind off Zoë and the way she moved and the way she smelled and the way she...never mind.

Now that he was fueled by sleep and energy, he had all kinds of self-control. He felt sure he could win that little battle, as well.

Tommy had led the expedition as all nineteen couples paddled canoes down the river that spilled out of Explorer's Lake, ending up on the very edge of the camp, where the river cut through some hills and a bridge crossed over high above their heads. So far, so good. He and Zoë managed to paddle just fine and keep their strokes even, although she'd never been in a canoe before.

They all dutifully trudged up to the top of the hill, to the side of the bridge.

"Today, we will ask you to take a risk," Tommy said with gusto. "We will ask you to trust your partner completely."

Jake groaned the minute he heard the word *trust*. He glanced at Zoë, and he could see it on her face, too. Trust was not a good topic for them. They always messed up the trust tests. Either he wouldn't follow her directions to assemble some stupid puzzle, or she couldn't let him lead her blindfolded down the balance beam, or neither was willing to fall backward and let the other catch them.

Whenever someone said "trust," it seemed the two of them flunked out.

And the fact that they were on top of a bridge, with wind blowing like crazy, and the river far below them, did not inspire confidence, either. They were probably going to ask them to walk a tightrope or dangle your partner upside down from the pylons or something equally scary, and he already knew Zoë wouldn't go for it. Jake shook his head. He wanted to win this one, but it didn't look good.

"What we are asking you to do, to show just how much you trust your partner, is double-bungee, right here, off the bridge," Tommy divulged. "This is not a test that one or the other can do. You both have to go, together. And as a special treat, the first couple that successfully jumps earns a special ride back to camp in a limo."

The prize sounded nice, but as "double-bungee" sunk in, several of the couples backed off right away. Jake, however, was feeling chipper. He had bungeed in the past with his brothers and he felt confident he could bungee again. Not so sure though about Zoë, but maybe he could persuade her.

"No way I'm that stupid," one man muttered with an edge of hysteria in his voice. "I'm an engineer. Do you know how unsafe that is? It's not about trusting my wife. It's about trusting you people to have properly calculated the coefficient of restitution of the elastic."

His obvious panic infected several others, and they scurried to join the "definite no" bunch.

Overachievers Ron and Tori, of course, stepped up, hand in hand. "We'll go first," she said brightly. "Where do we go?"

One of the counselors led the way to the middle of the bridge, where Tori practically threw herself into the harness. "I've always wanted to bungee. I'm so excited!"

Ron didn't look so sure. "Come on," she harangued, and he moved more slowly, but he did what he was told, sliding into the straps. He tested them, pulling this way and that, peering over the edge, judging the distance, backing off, peering again.

"The poor guy's hands are shaking," Jake noted.

Tori and Ron were bound together and maneuvered to the very lip of the bridge, onto a platform over the railing, ready to leap, as Ron teetered on the edge. He began to scream like a banshee. "No, no, I can't!" he shrieked. "Get me out of here! I can't!"

Tori had a few choice words for him, but before they scared off anyone else, they were hustled off the platform and to the other side of the bridge with the people who had already said they couldn't or wouldn't go.

"We've never had a group before where no one would bungee-jump," Tommy said with disgust. "What's wrong with you people?"

"We'll do it." Pulling Zoë along behind him, Jake emerged from the group.

"I'm afraid of heights," Zoë whispered, dragging on his hand. "I don't think I can do that."

"I've done it before. I know you, Zoë, and I know you're going to love it. No problem, Zoë. Really."

"You've done it before?" she asked, and he could see the fear in her face.

"Trust me, Zo. We can do this."

She nodded. "I do trust you. I do."

As they neared the middle of the bridge, Tommy scoffed, "You two? The flunkies? I don't think so."

"That's okay," Jake returned. "We think so, and we're the ones who count." He kept Zoë's hand firmly in his.

"You're sure, right?" Zoë murmured.

"I wouldn't ask you to do this unless I was sure." He inspected the equipment closer up, and verified for himself that it was okay. "You can close your eyes, okay?" he told her, as they were buckled in. "Just hang on to me and keep your eyes closed."

After they inched out on the platform, she ventured a tiny peek over the edge. "Oh, God, Jake," she said in a shaky voice, "this is going to be some giant whoosh, isn't it? Are you sure I can do this?"

"Yep. Totally sure. Just hang on."

"Hang on to you," she whispered, squeezing her eyes shut and wrapping her arms around him. "I can do that."

Jake grinned. He had no doubt Zoë was going to love this. He held her tight and leaned back, pulling them both over the edge, and hurtled them into space. Zoë's face was pressed into his shoulder, but when they started to fly, she tipped her head up enough to see him, and her eyes went wide.

She screamed so loud he was afraid he might never regain his hearing, but it was a good scream, the kind you make on a roller coaster. She was yelling and laughing and smiling at the same time, and Jake just held on for the ride.

It was a major, mind-blowing leap, the total feeling of flying, and then nothing but gently rolling around on the end of the cord, during which she was still hooting with delight. By the time they were finally unwrapped and detached from the cords and straps, Zoë was laughing so hard she could barely stand up.

Up above them, the other campers were cheering and clapping for them, leaning over the bridge, making "Woo-woo!" noises.

"That was the most fun ever," Zoë cried, bouncing up and down. "Can we do it again?"

"Not right this minute," he winced, testing his ribs where she'd squeezed a little too hard. But triumph overrode pain. They'd endured days of being the camp losers, but now they had won one! "It was fun, wasn't it? And we won, Zo. We won!"

"I know! And we did it together. Because I trusted you."

She stepped back, gazing at him with such adoration he couldn't believe it. No one had ever looked at him that way.

"Jake," she said, almost in awe, "I trust you."

"Yeah, you do." He smiled. "I trust you, too."

Laughing out loud, she tangled her arms around his neck, stretched up to slant her mouth across his and kissed him hard, hot and way over the top, jolting him down to his toes.

He knew it was just a spillover of adrenaline and he didn't care. He was feeling the same rush of reckless joy and heady exhilaration and incredible...love.

Love? He loved Zoë? Of course he did.

That realization knocked the wind out of his sails. But he couldn't think about that now. He'd been holding back his desire for so long—too long—and it was starting to spill out. And it felt *so* good. Irresistibly good. So he concentrated on kissing her back, looping his arms around her tight enough to lift her up into him, plunging inside her mouth, tasting and taking everything she had to offer.

"Excuse me," the EJ handler who'd helped them down interjected, tapping on Jake's shoulder. "Sorry to interrupt, but I wanted you to know that, since you were the first and maybe the only ones to successfully complete the bungee challenge, you two get a ride back to your cottage in the Humvee limo. They have champagne for you and everything." He pointed to the limo idling on the small road next to the river. "Right over there."

A Humvee limo. Who knew such a thing existed? If his mind had been clear, he might've cared. But Jake was beyond that.

Half dragging, half leading Zoë to the limo, Jake kept kissing her, laughing into her mouth, hanging on to her securely, until they ducked inside the door to the limo.

It was huge inside the thing, and there was a small bar set up with a bucket of champagne and two crystal flutes, plus a small basket of strawberries. A card tied with red ribbon to the bottle read, "Together Forever, No Matter What."

Jake sort of shoved her down into the back seat, and then he followed, hungrily kissing her again.

"I loved bungee-jumping," she murmured into his mouth, framing his face with her hands, sliding soft kisses over his chin and his jaw. "I loved the whole thing. And, oh Lord, Jake, I love you."

He stilled. "Zoë, I..."

She sat up a little, blushing slightly. "I'm sorry. I didn't mean to blurt it out like that," she hastened to say. "I don't know what I was—"

"No, no, it's okay," he said quickly. He settled his arms around her, making it clear he wasn't going to let her get too far away in the back seat. "In fact, it's great." He smiled, remembering the glow in her eyes when she'd said she trusted him, remembering the warmth in his heart when he'd realized how he felt. He shook his head, but it didn't go away. It was there in every beat of his heart. "I love you, Zoë. I don't know exactly when this happened, but there it is."

Her eyes searched his face. "You really mean that, Jake? You love *me?*"

"Absolutely." He leaned forward to slide open the partition between them and the driver. "Hurry, will you? We're on the hillside. Villa Number eleven." And then he closed it with a slam.

"Why the rush?" She nabbed a strawberry and started to nibble. "I kind of like the limo."

"Because as soon as I get you one step inside the door of that cottage," he said roughly, rolling her underneath him, "I'm going to make love to you in every way I can think of, for as long as I can make it last. I've been way too good for way too long. No more. I'm looking forward to being very, very bad."

She sucked in air so fast she almost swallowed the strawberry. Instead, she tossed it aside and reached for him. "Who says we have to wait for the cottage?"

12

IT WAS A BUMPY RIDE from the bridge to the cottage, and they made the most of every bump. Zoë had never fooled around in a moving vehicle, but they were both way too turned-on to just sit there and twiddle their thumbs. A few kisses, some well-placed touches, some zippers unzipped and strings unstrung and fabric pushed away. Neither wanted to take it all the way in the back of the limo, but they were willing to do enough to whet their appetites for the main course coming up.

And there was something really fun and outrageous about the gymnastics involved in maneuvering in and out of your clothes in such a tight space, as well as something exciting about not knowing where you, your hands, or your legs would end up if you hit a dip or a steep turn, if you fell off the seat and took someone else with you, if you spilled champagne and had to lick it off...something new around every curve.

She had to hand it to Jake. He may have held out a long time, but once he made up his mind, he definitely knew what to do. She'd barely touched him, but she was undressed and unencumbered and her body was already humming and thrumming before they got half-way to their cabin, as he applied his clever mouth and his deft hands to the exact spots that needed attention the most. If he hadn't clamped his hand firmly over her mouth, she would've already been screaming out his name, if for no other reason than the fact that he seemed bound and determined not to finish what he started. He would stroke her or kiss her until she was trembling, and then draw away.

One thing she had learned—Jake seemed to have a real talent for making her wait. "Damn it, Jake," she groaned. "I'm dying here."

"Not till we're inside the cottage," he said huskily. "One foot inside."

"One inch inside," she bargained.

She could feel his lips curve into a smile against her stomach, and she took that as a yes. One inch inside.

The second the Humvee pulled up on the trail outside the Hillside Villa Number eleven, Jake tugged her tank top down and slipped her pants up and tied the string. Then he whipped her around so she was facing away from him, and attached her firmly to the front of him. With his rigid length pressing into her back, he hastily navigated both of them up the steps. It was one very smooth covert operation.

"I don't think the driver cares," she murmured, lifting a hand behind her to pull his head down to her neck. "I'm sure he sees a lot of half-dressed, aroused people around this place."

He took the opportunity to nibble her neck and whisper in her ear. "Yeah, well, you and I are not just anybody, and I don't care who he is, I don't want him knowing our business."

"I hate to break it to you, but you left my underwear on the seat," she said demurely. "I think he'll have a fair idea of what we were doing."

But Jake shook his head, removing a scrap of pale-peach-colored lace from his jacket pocket. "You think I'd leave a souvenir like that for the limo driver? Not in this lifetime."

Zoë just kept smiling.

As he fiddled with the doorknob, she turned around in his arms so she could lean against the door, circle her arms around him, and look up at him. *He said he loves me.* It was powerful stuff. She traced the outline of his adorable lips with the tip of her finger. "You know, one of the first things I loved about you was your lips. I've memorized those lips. I see them in my dreams. Narrow on the top—" she dragged her thumb across "—and fuller on the bottom."

He bit down on her thumb. "Not my inseam? You seemed to like that when you couldn't take your hands off me on the bus. Or my butt? I thought you said I had a wonderful butt."

She swallowed. "That came later." How was it possible to have this many tingles and twitches so deep inside when all he was doing was gently sucking on her thumb? Oh, my, my.

Somehow, he managed to cover her mouth with his, kissing her thoroughly, playing a swift game of tango with her tongue, at the same time he rammed the door open, practically off its hinges. She stepped backward over the threshold, but she was dizzy and dazed, and she tripped. Tumbling down to the carpet, she landed with a thud, catching herself with both arms. Jake followed, coming inside just far enough to kick the door closed, and then he joined her on the floor, partially on top of her, relentlessly levering her into the floor.

"You promised one inch inside the door," she reminded him, already shoving away his jacket.

"And I always make good on my promises," he returned, peeling off his T-shirt, strewing clothing every which way in his haste to strip off her pants and get rid of his own.

His ended up around his ankles and her tank top only got halfway off, but they were too frantic to bother with details like that. Jake pinned her to the carpet, bonking her head against the edge of the leather chair, every bit as hungry and greedy as she was to feel skin on skin, heat on heat, silken limb clench around strong muscle.

She closed her eyes and sighed with the pure, giddy pleasure of it, wrapping her arms around him, bringing up her knees, trying to hold him closer, hurry him faster. It seemed impossible to feel as much as she wanted to feel, to drink in as much of Jake as she wanted to taste. But she was willing to give it a try, letting out a little moan as she rubbed her cheek against the top of his head, lifting herself, pressing up into his mouth and his hand. His fingers pinched and provoked one taut, sensitive nipple as he licked and bit the other through the thin fabric of her shirt, now wet from his mouth. Sensation and heat rippled through her, and she was beyond impatient, beyond eager.

"Now," she begged, running her fingers down his muscled torso, filling her hands with his sweat-slick, warm flesh. His ribs, his hipbones, around to the curve of that beautiful bottom. She pressed him up into her thighs, urging him toward the one spot they both desired, wanted, needed him to be.

"Not yet," he groaned, but she knew his control was as ragged as hers.

Delighting in her new power, she wiggled down, reaching between them, finding his velvety tip, testing her palm against it. Sliding her tongue into his ear, wrapping her whole hand around him to try to move him up and in, she murmured, "We're one inch inside the door. Now I want you inside me."

"That wasn't the deal."

"Yes," she said breathlessly, "it was."

"Uh-uh. The deal was..." He swooped, neatly capturing both her wrists in one of his, forcing her hands onto the floor over her head, well away from what she wanted to touch. "The deal was that once we were one inch inside the door, I wouldn't make you wait and I'd give you what you needed."

She tried to lift her hips off the floor, but he used his long, strong body to push her back down. "Come on, Jake, you know what I need."

"Yeah, I do," he whispered, brushing kisses all down the slope of her neck and shoulder, continuing to tweak her breast, just grazing it with caresses, making her jump and tremble. He moved over her then, and she sighed with relief, thinking he finally intended to slip inside, but he didn't.

Instead, he kept his hand on her breast, cupping her, teasing her nipple, as down below, he slid the tip of his manhood against her, barely grazing her, but in exactly the right spot, starting this amazing, crazy, uneven rhythm that seemed destined to drive her mad. Shocked, surprised, she couldn't fight it. She began to moan in earnest, unable to control herself as she arched against him. The insistent feel of his fingers, the irresistible motion of his hard, slippery flesh. She was so wet and ready, and there was no way to hold back.

"Damn you, Jake. Damn you," she cried out, reaching and shattering. This wasn't the way she wanted it to happen. But she shivered with the hard, fast pleasure of it, climaxing, coming apart at the seams whether she wanted to or not.

He was smiling, damn him, enjoying the shuddering aftereffects of his handiwork, and she wanted to smack him. Instead, she rolled over on top of him, catching him by surprise this time. Straddling him, she slipped down his length, moaning as she took all of him deep inside.

"Oh, yeah," she whispered, rocking up and down, just enough to make him have to fight to keep her pace. "My turn."

She tipped over, brushing her breasts against his chest, locking her knees against his hips, nipping at him for a kiss, keeping herself just out of reach, taunting him.

"Not fair," he gritted. But then he smiled. A tiger's smile. It should've warned her. Just when she thought she was in charge, he grabbed her and flipped her over in one fluid motion.

Holding her still, his hips poised between her thighs, he gazed down at her for a long pause, long enough to make her start to quiver again. And then he plunged inside.

Almost immediately, she could feel herself climbing again, and she couldn't believe it, wasn't sure she could take it. But, oh, yes, please, yes, she could.

It was a thing of beauty, staring into Jake's true-blue eyes as she felt him stroke deep and then deeper inside her, filling her again and again. She cried out his name, tangling her arms and legs around him, riding every exquisite tremor and tasting every wave of bliss.

Finding his own release, he sank against her, gasping for breath. "We didn't make it up to the jungle bed," he mumbled. "That damn bed. And we forgot about the condom jar and the chocolate paint."

"Next time?" she suggested.

"I like the way you think."

Exhausted, sated, amazingly content, Zoë yawned as

she lay there, cradled in his arms. "In a little while, I'll move," she murmured, listening to his heart beat under her ear. "Oh, I forgot to tell you, there's also a banana split you can order to eat in bed. Well, on the bed. Or off you."

Jake lifted his head. "Off me? You want to eat a banana split off me?"

Zoë smiled. "Oh, *yeah*."

MUCH LATER, after one large banana split, several condoms, and a very interesting stop about halfway up the stairs, Zoë and Jake had made it back to the big round bed.

Most of the sheets were on the floor, but she had retrieved a pillow, and she was lying on her stomach with her head crammed into the pillow, trying to rest up for the next round.

"I hate to make you move, but..." Jake sketched a path with a feather he'd found in the dresser, all the way from her shoulder blade to the bottom of her spine, swirling around, making her derriere twitch and rise up off the bed. "We never used the hot tub. I was wondering how you felt about maybe moving the party out there."

"The hot tub? You know, I had this great fantasy about you in that hot tub." She tipped over far enough to wink at him. "Every time I think I have to stop and take a breather, you pull me right back in. Because, you see, I want to find out if you, me and the hot tub is as good as my fantasy."

"Is that a challenge?"

"If you want it to be."

Throwing away the feather, he extended a hand. "I can take any challenge you throw down, darlin'."

She smiled. "I bet you can."

He leaped off the bed and raced down the stairs, not bothering with clothes, and she let him win that one, preferring to take a lazier path, sliding into the big, thick EJ robe, and bringing some towels with her, just in case the night air got chilly before they were ready to come in.

Jake was already in when she got there, his skin wet and gleaming, with swirling water and rising bubbles parting around him, revealing more than they covered. It was every bit as good as her vision. Even better. This was real.

Making a show of dropping her robe, taking her time, enjoying the gleam in his eye, she dipped one toe in the hot, bubbling water. And then she sloshed in all at once, sliding down his body, reveling in the evidence of his renewed desire, right there underneath her.

"Mmm," he said, nuzzling her neck. "Let's get out the bubble bath. It says you can use their own bubble bath in this thing, right? Bubbles could be fun."

Zoë stiffened. Bubble bath? During their long and luscious interlude, she had forgotten all about what was really going on at the Explorer's Journey, what with the aphrodisiacs hidden in all the toiletries.

She hesitated. Could she use the EJ drugged-up bubble bath? Would it hurt them? Gazing down at the pieces of Jake visible through the frothy water, she decided that she and Jake were doing fine on their own without any help from pharmaceuticals, and she preferred to just say no, thank you very much.

"Uh, no," she muttered. "No bubbles."

"Why not?" His fingers closed on her rib cage and he tickled her, making her squirm and giggle, stirring up the water. His grin was so cute and cheeky it made her heart go pitter-patter. "You know you want bubbles," he teased.

She sat back. "I thought the smell of the EJ products made you sick."

"I'm over it." But his eyes narrowed on her face. "You're acting weird, Zoë. What's going on?"

"Nothing." But after what they had shared, falling back on her old excuses seemed ridiculous. Not to mention disgusting. She knew every corner of his body, and he had taken her places she'd never dreamed of. It just wasn't right to lie to him, even by omission.

"Tell me," he ordered, drawing his brows together. "I hate secrets, especially between you and me."

She nodded. "I know. You're right. People who love each other don't keep things from each other." She bit her lip.

"And stop chewing on your poor lip. I like that lip," he murmured sweetly, and her heart turned over again. "Whatever it is, Zoë, we'll deal with it."

She hoped so. But this wasn't going to be easy. "There are a few things I should've told you before, but I just...I never found the right time," she said apologetically. "But I can't hold this back anymore. After what we've shared, I—I just have to tell you."

"So tell. Spit it out, will you?"

"Okay, so, first, about the bubble bath. You know how you thought everyone seemed, well, addicted to sex? You were right." That got his attention. Jake lurched up out the tub. "No, no, not us! I made sure all of it was out of our cottage. You stole soap and I stole some shampoo and—"

"What are you talking about? The soap and the shampoo?"

"Oh, come on, Jake. You had to notice! You got rid of

the soap, remember?'' she said plainly. ''Didn't you notice how turned-on you got every time you smelled me? Me, too! That damn coconut-pineapple-banana smell. Every hit I got a whiff, I wanted to jump you. It was overpowering. But that's not where *this* came from... Us, I mean. Because we were clean.''

''The soap? And the shampoo? All the EJ junk?'' He sat back down, hard, splashing water every which way. ''How stupid am I? This is so obvious.'' He glared at her. ''How long ago did you figure this out? Why didn't you tell me?''

''Not that long ago,'' she hedged. He had said he loved her and he'd proved it in the way he made love to her. Surely it was safe to tell him now? ''I—I didn't tell you because I was afraid you would leave. You know, go find some other cops or DEA agents or whoever would care that the Explorer's Journey is running some kind of sexual opium den.''

He got very quiet. All she could hear were the whooshing jets in the hot tub. ''First of all, we won't know until we have this stuff tested whether there is even anything illicit in it. For all we know, it's just coconut and pineapple and we're all operating under the power of suggestion. And second, I could get out, call the cops, and come back. Even before this,'' he said, sweeping his arm so she knew he meant her and him and the erotic playground they called a cottage. ''Even before I had another reason to stay, you knew I wouldn't leave as long as I was still looking for Toni.''

''Well, that's the second thing,'' she said delicately. ''I also knew that...'' She stopped.

''You're driving me crazy here. Just tell me! What?''

''Toni. She isn't here,'' Zoë blurted. ''She never was. I just pretended to still look for her because, well, like you said, because I thought you wouldn't leave if you still thought there was a possibility she was here."

"No Toni?" he demanded. "But how do you know that? How can you be sure?"

"Oh, Jake," she wailed, "you're making me tell you everything at once. I don't want to. Especially now. It's wrecking this whole fabulous thing we had going. And it has been so fabulous." Mournfully she added, "I guess I knew anything this good couldn't last."

Scooting out of the hot tub, she grabbed the robe and wrapped herself up securely. It just didn't feel right sitting there stewing, naked, while she confessed all the gory details.

"I have to be the world's biggest idiot," Jake whispered. "I'm clueless. They're stuffing some kind of magic sex dust in the soap, for God's sake, and I am a cop and I don't see it, but you do. And then you lie to me about it. I'm a good cop, damn it, and I'm completely fooled by little Miss Transparent!"

"I am not that transparent," she countered, tying the belt on her robe. "And it has nothing to do with you being a good cop. Okay, I'm not sure why you didn't figure out about the soap. Maybe because the fumes were messing with your mind." She shook her head. "It sure messed with my mind." As he started to object, she cut him off. "Let me finish. I need to say this now, while you're already cranky, because if you're being nice to me and I'm all head over heels in love with you like usual, I will never tell you. The truth is, Jake..." She swallowed. "The truth is that I am positive Toni is not and never was here because..." She held her breath. "Because I'm psychic."

His face was a study in disbelief.

She pushed on, anyway. "When you showed me the

picture, I knew she was the woman who got into a fight with her husband and never got on the bus. Do you remember?" He didn't answer, so she finished lamely, "At O'Hare. She's the one in the photo. I don't know how I knew it. I just did."

"Good God, Zoë." He stood up and she had to look away, because she could not see naked Jake and have any resolve whatsoever. Reduced to a blubbering idiot, she'd just tell him whatever he wanted to hear. So she stared at the wood of the deck floor, as he demanded, "You expect me to believe this?"

"In my own defense, you have to admit, in your heart, you knew she wasn't here," she argued. "We haven't had a single clue to link her to anyone in this camp."

"That's true," he muttered.

"And as for the psychic thing, it's not like I can help it," she protested, starting to lose her temper. "I knew about Toni, I knew about you for the empathy test, I knew that Toni wasn't here, and I knew you were the right man to come with me on this journey because I suddenly got psychic. Not really, really psychic, just slightly."

"Slightly?" he echoed, staring at her as if she'd lost her mind.

"Well, yes. It never happened before." She lifted her hands in the air. "But remember that tarot card that kept falling out the night you came to my apartment? It was the True Love card. That card jumped out at me twice, and I knew you were my true love, that it was meant to be." She wasn't making any headway here, but she kept trying. She had to make him understand. "I shouldn't have lied, I realize that, but I could see right through you. There was no way you were going to believe me and come along and play honeymoon just because the two of hearts jumped out."

Jake ran a rough hand through his hair. "You insisted on coming with me because of a *card?*" he asked savagely. "And you didn't want to tell me that, or about the allegedly sexually addictive soap, or about someone who may have been Toni ditching before she ever got on the trip, all because you were afraid I would leave? Desperate, crazy woman, clinging to a man she doesn't know? Have I got the whole thing now?"

"Yes, but..." Zoë met his gaze, trying to be strong. "But I know now that you love me and even though you *can* leave, you won't." She lifted her chin. "I trust you."

"Good for you." But Jake climbed out of the heart-shaped hot tub, dripping as he stalked across the deck and shoved open the sliding glass door.

Zoë slowly followed, trying to catch her breath. "It's okay," she told herself. "It's better that he knows it all now."

By the time she made it to the living room, he was coming down the stairs wearing his jeans and a T-shirt without the Explorer's Journey logo, and he was carrying his duffel bag.

"I'm going to see if I can hitch a ride on one of the delivery trucks," he said tersely. "I need to get some of these products to a lab and see what's in them."

He stomped out the front door, walking right over the spot where they'd first made love, leaving Zoë standing all alone in the honeymoon cottage.

ONCE HE REACHED an actual town, Jake tried to get his bearings. His cell phone wasn't working, so he couldn't call and check in or do anything useful, but he did find out from a friendly trucker where he was. How strange.

He'd felt as if he was on another planet, but he was actually only an hour or two from the fishing cabin where he was supposed to meet his brothers before all this nonsense began.

Sean and Cooper were probably frying up some walleye right now. He hoped so. It would be a major relief to walk into the cabin, smell frying fish, have somebody toss him a beer. Like returning to Earth.

But when he finally got there, walking partway and hitching the rest, he found the cabin was empty. No Sean. No Cooper. No fish. Although there was beer in the fridge. And also a couple of cartons of strawberries. Zoë's favorite food. The only answer he got right on the stupid empathy test.

"What the...?" Why would there be strawberries here? He stood there, with the refrigerator door open, staring at the shelves. Finally he grabbed a beer and slammed the door on the damn berries, wandering outside to look at the lake as he drank his beer.

Things had changed since the last time he was here. Someone had hung a hammock out under the tree, near the lake, and there was now a big sideways *N* carved into the tree.

"Okay, so it's a Z," he snapped. "I'm not stupid. So Zorro was here. It has nothing to do with Zoë."

But every time he turned around, there was something that reminded him of Zoë. If it wasn't the strawberries, it was the hammock, or that damn Z carved into the tree. What next? Tarot cards and bungee jumpers dropping out of sky? A Humvee limo parked out back?

He tramped back inside, dragged out the strawberries and then started flinging them into the lake, one at a time, swearing increasingly exotic curse words as he threw them. It didn't make him feel any better.

But after stewing a bit longer, knocking back a few more beers, Jake was getting ready to face facts.

"Nothing else to do," he groused. His cell phone still wasn't picking up a signal, but there was a phone in the cabin, so he dialed home. It was tough to do, but if Zoë could play True Confessions with him, then he could sure scare up a few words for his dad.

"You find her?" Michael Calhoun asked right off the bat.

"No." Jake let himself take a short pause. "She's not there. She was never on this tour."

"Damn it, I thought I could count on you," his father shot back. "You get your butt home, Jake. We'll have to circle the wagons, see if we can come up with a Plan B."

Plan B was to rip off your clothes and pretend you were making love. But his dad didn't know that.

"Yeah, yeah, okay. I'll be there as soon as I can find a way." But it didn't matter. He felt like dirt. Like less than dirt. "I did stumble into something else. It may be nothing, but the camp where she was supposed to go had some funny stuff going on. So I've got some things to send to a lab."

"So you didn't have your mind on my Toni problem, in other words." There was a snort over the line. "You were too busy fooling around with this other thing."

"I'm sorry, Dad," he mumbled. "It was never my intention to let you down."

Silence greeted him. Finally his dad put in, "Nothing I can say now, Jake. Everybody lets somebody down sooner or later. That's life." And he hung up.

Yeah, but not me, Jake wanted to argue. *I never let people down.*

Not him? That was a joke. Not only had he completely dropped the ball on the investigation for his father, but he had slept with Zoë, shared his heart with Zoë, and then walked out on her. He'd walked out on Zoë, knowing full well that watching someone she loved walk away from her was the one thing she feared most.

And not just anyone. The love of her life. Was that what he was? She'd called him her true love. Was he the love of her life? She sure felt like the love of his.

"Jeez, I hit the daily double. Took down my biggest fear and her biggest fear, all in the same day," he said roughly, gulping beer to ease the pain. "And all in all, I would say that disappointing Zoë makes me feel a hell of a lot worse than disappointing dear old Dad."

He ambled outside, taking another beer with him. Almost sunset. Pretty. He couldn't help but think about that hammock strung up outside Villa Number eleven. They never got to use it the way it was intended. Instead, she knocked him out of it and fell on top of him. And half fell out of her robe while she was at it.

His lips curved into a smile. That was fun.

Hammock. A big Z. Strawberries. Plan B. Zoë everywhere he turned.

"Maybe there is something to this karma thing," he whispered, wondering what Zoë was up to. Was she pining away all by herself in couples' paradise? Had she hitched a ride out, too, rather than face the humiliation of being a *one* in a camp full of *twos*?

Wherever she was, was she feeling wounded and heartbroken because he had walked away?

Suddenly he couldn't stand the idea of Zoë being unhappy. So what if she picked up on clues he didn't? That was just pettiness and pride talking. So what if she thought she was psychic? If she thought that, she probably had her reasons. Who was he to tell her she wasn't?

So what if she'd lied to him? She was right about his

reaction, wasn't she? The minute she'd told him the truth, he'd bolted, like the irresponsible jackass she was afraid he would turn out to be. After Wylie, the last thing Zoë needed was one more jerk running out on her.

"Time to step up and be a man, Jake," he yelled at himself. "Who are you? You're the sure thing, remember? The guy who always stands up."

He raced back in and picked up the phone. Before his father had a chance to say hello, Jake announced, "Listen, Dad, I'm not coming back right away. There's something I have to take care of first. I'll see you. Maybe in a week. Maybe longer."

He could hear his dad protesting, but he hung up anyway. Life was too short to waste time. Right now he could've been watching the sunset in a hammock with Zoë.

It took a while to hitch a ride to Eau Clair, find a friendly delivery man headed for the Explorer's Journey who didn't mind sneaking in an extra passenger, and then hoof it all the way back down one hill and up another, but he had incentive. He was on his way to see Zoë, to hold her and touch her and promise never to leave again. Finally he was there, standing in front of Villa Number eleven with his hands in his pockets, hoping he could make this work.

He didn't bother to go in the front door, just cut through the underbrush around to the back. He could tell before he got there that she was curled up in the hammock, just where he knew she'd be.

He got as far as the edge of the deck before she saw him coming. Blushing furiously, she scrambled to sit up, which never did work in the hammock.

He offered a hand. She shook her head. So there he

was, trying to make his apologies and mend fences while she half reclined in a hammock.

"I'm sorry," he said gruffly. "I shouldn't have left. I love you. I should've stayed. We should've fought it out. That's what people who love each other do. They don't walk away."

Zoë was chewing her lip.

"Are you going to say anything or not?" he demanded. "And don't do that to your lip. I..." He smiled. "I like your lips."

"Jake, you drive me nuts," she declared. "I thought you'd never get here. I have been so bored. You can't even play solitaire in this stupid place. All the cards have naked people on them."

Jake's smile widened. "So you forgive me?"

"Forgive you? I love you!" Her lips curved into one of her warmest, most glowing smiles, and Jake felt the impact down to his shoes. "Jake," she added, "I'm sorry to ask that, but could you please come over here and get me out of this ridiculous hammock? I'm stuck, and I would really like to kiss you now."

He was there in a heartbeat, lifting her into his arms, holding her tight enough that he hoped she understood he would never let her go again.

"I knew you'd be back," she said, but there was enough of an edge to her voice that he knew she wasn't that sure. "I knew it all along. It was destiny, Jake."

"Yep," he whispered back. "Destiny."

* * * * *

Look for Book 2 in the
True Blue Calhouns *miniseries*
by popular Julie Kistler,
coming in February 2003!

Cut to the Chase

By the third day, Sean Calhoun had her routine down cold. She would show up on the Quad in early morning or late afternoon, ridiculously overdressed, carefully buttoned into that damn coat, wearing some sort of hat and her sunglasses. She would sit under the same maple tree, eat an amazing amount of crackers and other snacks, stare into space, and look anxious or upset from time to time.

Nice profile, good nose, excellent smile, beautiful skin. Fondness for baseball, given the White Sox bag and the Orioles cap she had on today, and a major taste for saltine crackers, grapes, cheese curls, muffins and milk. Especially the crackers.

Man, he was in bad shape—slipping from surveillance ever closer to plain old stalking—if he was reduced to keeping track of everything she ate. What was it about her he found so damn fascinating? And why was he hoping against hope she wasn't the woman he was supposed to locate?

"No way this girl was fooling around with my old man," he said grimly from his vantage point behind the front doors of Lincoln Hall.

But his analysis of the situation was interrupted when she suddenly bolted up from where she was sitting, abandoning her snacks and her tote bag, careening off toward a secluded area near the English building and looking a little green around the gills. Without a second's hesitation, Sean followed.

He caught up to her where she'd stopped to hang on to a tree trunk for dear life. She'd lost her sunglasses, her hat had fallen off a few feet away, and she was tossing her cookies into the grass like there was no tomorrow.

Pale, shaky, unsteady, she turned. Her gaze met Sean's.

Wow. Her eyes were hazel. Even under these circumstances, they were beautiful and warm. Very warm. She paused, blinked, still focused on him, as if she were trying to figure out who he was and what he was doing there. He had never felt so awkward and yet so instantly connected to anyone in his life.

Sean edged nearer, picking up the baseball cap. "Sorry," he said quietly. "I don't mean to intrude. But I could tell you were..."

And that was when he finally put two and two together. The bulky clothes, the saltines, the sudden nausea...

Abra Holloway was pregnant.

"Go away," Abra said flatly.

The last thing she needed at this moment was some nosy stranger trying to interfere. He didn't look dangerous, just way too cute for his own good, with light brown hair cut short and shoved carelessly to one side, and an intense, serious expression on his face. Wearing a white T-shirt and faded blue jeans, he seemed like a regular guy. Or at least an extremely good-looking regular guy. Wide shoulders, nice muscles, lean hips... Yum.

But a snoop was still a snoop, no matter how hunky the package. She spared him another glance and immediately wished she hadn't. He was adorable, whoever he was, standing there, looking all concerned.

Abra groaned, hanging on tight to the tree, wishing her stomach would stop this topsy-turvy stuff. She'd eaten every saltine in sight and she still felt absolutely miserable. "I said, go away," she repeated.

But he shook his head, still advancing on her. "I want to help," he said kindly. "For one thing, I think we should get you out of that hot coat."

Before she could move away, he was right there, gently holding her steady as he unwound her from the coat and folded it over his arm. Great. A *chivalrous* snoopy hunk.

"Better?" he asked in that same soothing, annoying tone, laying his palm on her forehead as if she were a three-year-old with a temperature, and she wanted to smack him.

"Yes, that is better, thank you, but..."

But I'm supposed to be in disguise, and now my hat and my sunglasses and even my nice, baggy coat are gone, and all that's left is Abra Holloway, media star, with ugly dyed brown hair and a bad case of the heaves. And you are way too cute to be standing there staring at me while I toss my cookies!

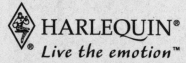

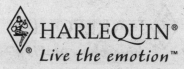

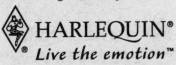

eHARLEQUIN.com

Becoming an eHarlequin.com member is easy, fun and **FREE!** Join today to enjoy great benefits:

- **Super savings** on all our books, including members-only discounts and offers!

- Enjoy **exclusive online reads**—FREE!

- Info, tips and **expert advice** on writing your own romance novel.

- FREE romance **newsletters,** customized by you!

- Find out the latest on your **favorite authors.**

- Enter to win exciting **contests and promotions!**

- Chat with other members in our **community message boards!**

Plus, we'll send you 2 FREE Internet-exclusive eHarlequin.com books (no strings!) just to say thanks for joining us online.

To become a member, visit www.eHarlequin.com today!

INTMEMB

If you're a fan of sensual romance you *simply* must read…

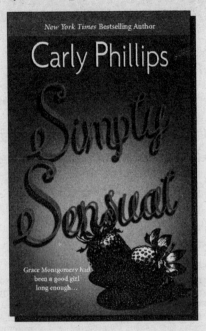

New York Times Bestselling Author

Carly Phillips

Simply Sensual

Grace Montgomery had been a good girl long enough…

The third sizzling title in Carly Phillips's *Simply* trilogy.

"4 STARS—Sizzle the winter blues away with a *Simply Sensual* tale…wonderful, alluring and fascinating!"
—*Romantic Times*

Available in January 2004.

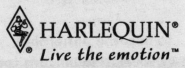

HARLEQUIN®
Live the emotion™

Visit us at www.eHarlequin.com

PHSSCP3